ROMANCE IN MY COFFEE

ROMANCE IN MY COFFEE

ANDALEEB WAJID • ANURAG BANERJEE
ARAVIND JAYAN • GANKHU SUMNYAN
JERRY PINTO • K VAISHALI
MEERA GANAPATHI • NISHA SUSAN
RIDDHI DASTIDAR • SUNITI NAMJOSHI

EDITED BY
APARNA KAPUR

HarperCollins *Publishers* India

First published in India by HarperCollins *Publishers* 2025
HarperCollins *Publishers* India, Cyber City, Building 10-A,
Gurugram, Haryana – 122002, India

www.harpercollins.co.in

2 4 6 8 10 9 7 5 3 1

P-ISBN: 978-93-7307-574-7
E-ISBN: 978-93-7307-888-5

Cover design by Bonita Shimray

Typeset in 13/19.5 Adobe Jenson Pro
by HarperCollins *Publishers* India Pvt. Ltd

Printed and bound at
Saurabh Printers Pvt.Ltd (India)

MIX
Paper
FSC FSC® C010615

This book is produced from independently certified FSC® paper to ensure responsible forest management.

HarperCollins Publishers, Macken House, 39/40 Mayor Street Upper,
Dublin 1, D01 C9W8, Ireland

Contents

Under the Devil's Tree

Riddhi Dastidar

It happened as momentous things often happen, with no forewarning or good reason. The 50m sprinter on Nile was struck down by a lateish-in-life case of chickenpox. The inter-house track meet was less than a month away. Annie needed to be more a part of things anyway, the PT teacher said. She was their only option, her housemates said.

They surrounded her one recess. 'Think of the house spirit,' one girl said.

'We were literally assigned by roll number,' Annie said.

They left her then to confer amongst themselves and at the end of the school day, she was passed a note: 'JOIN THE TEAM OR UR JOURNAL GETS IT <3'

'Really, guys? Grow up.'

But one of them held up an exacto knife against its flimsy brown paper, until she rolled her eyes and went with them to the housemistress.

'See you for practice tomorrow. 7:30 a.m. Don't be late!'

ANNIE

moved her beans around the plate at dinner, until her mother lost patience.

'Tick tick one, Annie.'

Annie stuffed all five into her mouth at once.

'I have to go early tomorrow to school,' she mumbled as she cleared the table.

'What for?'

'They need a substitute for track. Runner got chickenpox.'

Her mother's eyes widened in shock though she recovered quickly. 'Wow, Anniepie. Tell Papa. He'll be really pleased.'

Annie shrugged. 'Jaga dena please, six o'clock,' she said, going into her room and shutting the door behind her.

Her mother followed her. 'All good?' she asked.

Annie shrugged again. 'Of course,' she said. 'Why wouldn't it be?'

Her mother surveyed her for a second, dissatisfied. She settled for a kiss on the forehead. 'Don't stay up too late then. I don't know how all that stuff doesn't give you nightmares.'

Annie pressed play on *Nightmare on Elm Street* before her mother had even left the room.

ZEE

cycled to school earlier than usual that day. Much too early for morning training; it was only 7 a.m. She just couldn't trust herself to spend time around Kamna yet in the carpool. She needed some time to prepare herself. A pre-warm-up warm-up, some time to herself would do her good. Sweat it out, her mum always said. Great advice.

She was doing a lazy lap around the field when she noticed another figure at the base of the tallest tree in the perimeter. She jogged over, and the girl looked up from the journal in her hand, watching her approach. Her face was suspicious behind her big brown glasses.

It was only Loony. No, hor—fuck, what was her actual name?

'It's Annie,' the girl said.

'Annie!' Zee smiled. 'I know. Obviously.'

'Do you?' She sounded combative.

'What're you doing here so early?'

'I could ask you the same question,' Annie said.

'It's morning sports practice.'

'Same pinch,' Annie said.

'O-kay.' Mystifying but Annie didn't seem inclined to elaborate. She looked at Zee warily instead, like she was waiting for her to leave. *Her* field. The nerve of this weirdo. Her journal lay open on her lap. Zee could see the beginnings of a sketch of a bunch of leaves and something scribbled in indecipherable handwriting. Annie saw Zee looking and slammed her journal shut.

'I'm outtie,' Zee said, jogging away. Bizarre. Other students were starting to stream in now. Zee waved at the coach and did a spontaneous handstand. She was very proud of it, actually. It had taken her months to master. Her friends clapped across the field. She swept a glance over—that weird girl was still looking at her. Whatever.

By the end of morning practice it was clear Annie hadn't been lying. She was doing exercises (pretty decent form actually) with the others in Nile house at their end of the track. Who knew. The bell rang for homeroom and the girls streamed in, red cheeks, baby hairs flying. The smell of sweat mingled with the orange tang of Glucon-D wafting out of water bottles as they walked into school.

ANNIE

spent a lot of time thinking about how to get elsewhere. At home—when her father was home—her parents fought with each other, trading sentences that were serrated. Annie tuned most of it out.

They had an LGBTQIA+ and allies session for parents at school, which her mother attended enthusiastically. Annie wondered how proudly she would display the ally bracelet if she knew that Annie liked girls. She thought she'd spare her this one for a while longer. It's not like she was in any danger of developing a girlfriend. A friend to begin with—that would be nice. One single friend. Even that felt like asking for the moon. Why was Zee of all people talking to her? Why had she even shown up so early, intruding on her space?

Day One practice had gone decently. For the time being, she had social interaction. Her mother would be so relieved. She didn't mind track, actually. The more she ran, the faster she became. She knew what lay down this road—timing herself obsessively, shedding layers to be even more lightweight. It was something else to do. Feeling the wind speed in your ears was good. Beating girls who had made your life hell was better.

'Maybe this will fix your posture,' her mother said to her at dinner. Papa was working late again, thank goodness. 'I hate how you hunch. It smacks of low self-confidence.'

Annie sat up extra-straight in her chair and pulled an exaggerated smile at her mother. All teeth.

'All right, smarty-pants, put that away.'

The next two morning practices, Annie and Zee spotted each other and avoided each other till the rest showed up. Zee stretched on one side of the field, and did not go anywhere near Annie. Annie continued with her observation and recording.

ZEE

woke up too early and reached for her phone immediately. She needed to stop refreshing K's finsta. She needed to block her actually, but instead she compulsively checked back in every few hours. What if she had made a second finsta?

Get a grip, Zee told herself. Sweat it out. It's only 6 a.m. You can still rescue this day. Soon she was on her cycle, pedalling and not thinking about anything but directions to school. There was Loony, no ... *Annie* again. A distraction! Zee seized it.

'You do know you're early for morning practice, right?' she said.

Annie looked up, scowling. 'What's it to you? I'm not bothering you.'

Zee tried again. 'See, you're sketching the leaves, right? What if I got you a closer look?'

Before Annie could say anything, she'd shimmied up the tree and was hanging off a branch. Annie shrieked, 'Be careful,' but Zee was hanging upside down. Showing off a bit, it's true. In a moment though, she was back down, feet on the ground, with a mid-sized stem erupting in a cluster of five rounded leaves. She held it out to Annie.

Their fingers brushed briefly and Annie twitched. 'Thank you,' she said, taking the stem, and then she cracked the smallest smile.

'Truce?' Zee asked.

'Truce for what?'

'You know ... for calling you—for being a dumbass.'

'We'll see,' Annie said, but her smile was bigger. And her eyes, Zee noticed, behind her thick frames, were a deep chocolate brown.

'So why are *you* early for morning practice?' Annie said.

'Oh ... you know.' Zee pulled up a clump of grass. 'What about you?'

'I'm on lookout,' Annie said. 'Waiting for the day I get lucky.'

Zee sniggered and immediately regretted it. Annie's face had drawn shut. Shit.

'I need some alone time, to gather myself, before Kamna—my ex-girlfriend—and the rest show up. And I get too crazy at home because I wake up too early,' Zee said.

'Breakups are rough,' Annie said, her voice neutral.

'Yeah, yeah. So what are you on the lookout for?'

'There's a pair of hornbills who come to roost in this tree sometimes. I saw them once. Now I'm waiting to catch them again. Early mornings are the best bet for birds. Before it gets noisy,' Annie said.

'You a birder?'

'Not really. I just like weird things,' Annie said.

Zee couldn't tell if she was joking or not. That was the thing with Annie. She could say something normal but she didn't seem to ever make life any easier for herself. She looked at Zee now with big eyes through her big frames till Zee looked away.

In class that day, Zee looked over at Annie a few times. She sat several rows ahead, in the front right corner of the classroom. Right by the window. Even now, she was looking outside instead of paying attention to the maths lesson. Three rows behind her Kamna bent her head over her register. She was very good at maths. Zee looked up and caught Annie's eye. She quickly looked back at her work.

ANNIE

often wished she lived in a slasher movie. A really cosy one with a nice synthy soundtrack like *Nightmare* or *Friday the 13th* or even *Halloween*. In *Scream* she would obviously be Randy, minus the good old-fashioned misogyny-lite. In *Carrie,* she would probably be Carrie.

School was a long period of waiting it out until she could go to college, where even the weird girls met other weird girls. She would grow out her leg hair, dye her head hair and get a septum ring. She couldn't wait to grow up. School was taking forever. This month was taking forever. Why was November endless? The year dragged its feet after Diwali. She was extra sleepy these days after morning track practice, and she crashed out after lunch every day now. She loved waking up to her fairy lights in the window and the darkness outside.

She was almost done with her sketch of the saptaparni flowers and leaves. She looked at the stem she had propped up on her desk. Strange, she thought. She felt an odd twinge.

ZEE

didn't like how early the sun set these days. It added to the gnawing feeling in her stomach that seemed like it would swallow her up if she wasn't careful. She missed Didi so much. Why did she have to go to college halfway across the country? What was wrong with good old DU? She sat in her bedroom feeling sorry for herself over her sister's abandonment, Eggy's sudden death in February and then Kamna's betrayal a few months ago. Now it was getting colder again, and she couldn't help but think of Eggy. Everyone leaves in the end.

Her mother came in to find her crying in a dark room. 'Zoya,' she said, turning the lights on. 'Kya hua?' Zee was so worked up by then she couldn't speak. She howled and clung to her mother. 'Ohho bachhe,' her mother said, rocking her closer. 'Aaja, let's get you something to eat.'

At night Zee woke up to pee and discovered that she had bled through her pyjamas.

ANNIE

felt like her lungs would give out any second. Her throat was on fire. She still had two more rounds to go before she could collapse. 'Let's go, no slacking,' the housemistress called, clapping her large hands. One more. 'Last round, come on Annie, Rhea. Let's go!'

Annie finished and collapsed on the grass. It was prickly under her hands and neck. Her glasses were fogged up. She waited for her breathing to return to normal. Her vision was dark, dotted with bright spots. Next to her, Rhea muttered, 'I'd like to see *her* bloody go.'

As they got closer, practice became more intense. Annie was surprisingly into it. Some of the girls in her house had even become ... if not exactly friends, friendly. 'See you tomorrow, Anns,' Rhea said, clapping her on the shoulder. 'Maybe she can push us to a miraculous premature heart attack.'

Annie laced up her sneakers and scanned the field. She looked for Zee but she wasn't there. At recess she saw Zee hanging with her usual group in the quad. Her mouth was turned down. She looked ... subdued. It's not like they were friends. It's not like Annie could just go up and ask, 'Is everything okay?' Or like hold her hand or anything. What? Stop it, Annie.

Zee was Zee. Annie had made the grave mistake of doing an excessively enthusiastic presentation on hornbills last year. So they had a rude nickname for her now. It wasn't even the first one but it was the worst. Yeah right, Annie, she told herself. Get a bloody grip.

ZEE

bicycled to school early the next morning. She saw the familiar figure at the end of the field under the saptaparni and went over. 'Hey,' she said.

Annie smiled. 'How are you doing? Didn't see you yesterday.'

'Yeah, I was ... not doing super great.'

'Were you sick?'

'Oh you know. The usual once-a-month sickness.'

'Ah. Yeah. I finished my sketch, by the way. The close-up was very helpful. Thank you.'

'No problem. So you're … really into nature, huh?'

'I don't know. I like looking at things,' Annie said.

'Yeah, yeah. No offence but that's why people started calling you Creepy that one year,' Zee said.

Annie blanched. Somewhat diffidently she said, 'I know, I don't mean to stare.'

'And the not talking doesn't help.'

'Wow, did you just show up early to take a shit on me?'

'Oh … come on. I didn't mean it like that.'

'Great,' Annie said. 'Amazing, thanks.' And she jogged away. Zee watched her do a lap.

ANNIE

was not crying, not in front of people. Everyone was streaming in. She ran faster and the chill in the air stung her face. Serves you right, she told herself. She ran so fast, her housemates and the coach had to call to her several times to stop, to come for warm-up.

Someone was yelling, 'You'll hurt yourself!' She ran and ran, she couldn't even see their faces. Finally, she fell on the ground. Looking up at the sky she thought she finally spotted one of the hornbills. Though she could have been wrong. Again.

Zee

knew she had messed up. At recess she went looking for Annie, realizing that although they had been in the same section for the last five years, she had not the faintest idea of what the map of the school looked like for her. What did she do at recess? Hang in the quad with her friends? What friends? Hide in the library? Go camp under that goddamn tree? She spent all of recess looking, and right as the bell rang for biology, she saw that Annie was in her own seat, hunched over her journal. Uneasily she did a quick sweep of the classroom then went over.

'I'm really sorry, Annie,' she whispered. 'I was in a mood and I didn't mean it.'

Annie looked up at her. Her face was blank. 'Your friends are coming,' she said.

Back at her desk Nikki elbowed her in the ribs. 'What're you talking to Loony about?'

'Oh just passing a message from the coach,' Zee said. 'Did you do the assignment?'

ANNIE

felt every period in the second half of school like an entire day. The hours crawled by.

'Don't forget, we're staying back for practice,' someone from her house told her.

Annie breathed in, and out. 'You are a Final Girl,' she told herself fiercely. 'You will not be defeated.'

ZEE

felt like she had made amends. It was more than was expected of her. Come on, she had sought her out in front of everyone.

'Look, Loony's talking to herself again,' someone said behind her. Why couldn't Annie just be normal for two minutes? She remembered the year when Annie first got her nickname. Seventh grade. She really did talk to herself ... mutter, rather. Noticeably. She had stopped in eighth grade but not before the name stuck. Not before the teachers were nasty and pointed it out in front of everyone. She wondered now for the first time why Annie did it in the first place, and what had made her stop.

ANNIE

was doing arm-circles, waist rotations, alternate toe-touches. She was doing jumping jacks. She was doing squats. She was doing tag-sprints. She was doing laps. She was holding a plank. She was doing fifteen laps of the ground, alternating between a slow jog and a sprint. Annie was getting into position for the relay—third runner. She had really improved in these past weeks, enough to be more than adequate and not slow down their pace. The Nile housemistress was very pleased.

She stood with the games master, looking over at Annie and discussing something. It seemed ominous. Rhea broke her reverie. 'What did you do?'

Annie shrugged. 'No clue, man.'

'Girls, we have a proposition. We're going to switch it up a bit,' the games master said, walking over.

The girls looked at each other.

'Annie, we want you to be the closer.'

The girls looked at each other. Rhea chucked Annie on the arm.

'No, it's too crucial,' Annie stammered. 'How can we do this last minute?'

'It's far enough away. And you're improving in leaps and bounds. In fact, I don't know why you stopped running track in the first place,' the games master said, frowning. 'I remember I always used to pick you among the first five.'

That was exactly why Annie had quit. In eighth grade she used to be part of the school track team.

She was a sprinter back then, with the great encouragement of her father, who had been part of the Ranji team in his day. It was the last time he had taken an interest in her achievements. It was a bad summer, just before Annie got put on medication. She was already being bullied for mumbling to herself, unable to understand how her own brain could scare her so, unfamiliar with the concept of intrusive thoughts or compulsive behaviours. An off-putting whisper about the games master's nefarious reasons for favouring her had spread among some of the girls. Every time he called her name or beckoned her over, sniggering would break out, and sly looks exchanged. She started missing morning practice. Then she stopped going entirely. Her father blamed her mother, of course.

Now Annie looked at the other girls. They didn't seem upset. 'That's a great idea. No one will see it coming. Zip those lips,' Sahar, who had been the closer, said and winked.

Annie mimed zipping her lips.

'All right,' the housemistress said, clapping. 'Let's go!'

ZEE

could feel her heartbeat in her ears and in her throat. She breathed from her nose, exhaling slowly, then inhaling. Steady on, hero, she told herself. Being a distance runner meant having endurance, and if there was one thing she excelled at, it was the long haul.

She ran on the treadmill. The only thing that made her stop thinking these days—of Kamna, of Eggy—was running. She was beginning to feel light-headed. Maybe she was overdoing it. It had been morning, then afternoon. Perhaps another stretch in the evening would be too much.

Upstairs, her room waited in her flat, empty.

ANNIE

saw Zee after a week that morning. They had stayed out of each other's way. Zee waved at her as she walked over. November was a cold month. The air was heavy with smoke and laden with particles that made the field seem extra foggy.

'Are you going to be able to see your hornbills through all this?' Zee asked.

'That's what I'm worried about,' Annie said.

Neither of them mentioned the gap in meetings. 'How've you been?' Zee said.

'I finished my sketch of the devil's tree,' Annie said. She pointed at the tall tree above them, laden with white and green clusters of flowers.

'The saptaparni?' Zee asked.

'Yeah. *Alstonia scholaris*—because its bark is used to make blackboards. It's also called the devil's tree, shaitaan ka jhaad, which is why I'm into it.'

'Why?'

'Good question. I've tried looking this up but I've not found much. Apparently, ghosts and evil spirits reside in saptaparni. You're not supposed to pass under it.'

Zee laughed. 'But you spend so much time under it.'

'I'm really hoping to meet a ghost or a spirit,' Annie said seriously, and then she smiled back.

Something twisted in Zee's stomach. 'Um,' she said, 'right. Of course you do.'

'When I was young, my Dadu used to tell me stories about the shakchunni and the petni—Bengali like, tree-witches, or no, more like different kinds of female spirits—anyway my mother always told him to knock it off, but I think that's where I got my love for horror from. They were all my bedtime stories, and dinner-time stories. I was a slow eater and he was the only one who had enough patience to sit with me for hours.'

'That's really sweet. I don't know mine very well. They live in Canada with my chachu,' Zee said. 'Also I think they wish I was more girly.'

Annie scoffed. 'Ridiculous, you're perfect,' she said.

Zee looked at her. Annie looked back. They were suddenly tongue-tied, both flushing.

'Sorry,' Annie said. 'I didn't, I didn't mean it like that.' The doors in her eyes were closing, Zee could see, and she felt an answering almost physical twinge.

'No, listen. Do you want to hang out sometime?'

'What do you mean?' Annie said.

'I don't know. You said you like spooky things. I don't know much about it but there's a new *Final Destination* movie in theatres. You want to be my guru?'

Annie looked uncertain. 'Are you serious?'

'Yeah!'

'Why?'

'What do you mean why?'

'Why do you suddenly want to hang out?' Annie said. 'I know how you and your friends think of me.'

'Oh, come on. Don't people get second chances? I think you're cool, I want a change of scene from the shitshow that is my life right now. We're becoming friends. Right? This is how you make friends?'

'Okay,' Annie said. Then she smiled again, a big smile, and Zee felt that not-entirely-unpleasant twinge again.

'I'll text you,' Zee said. The others were slowly coming onto the field. Shit, she thought, jogging over to her housemates.

ANNIE

couldn't read, couldn't eat, couldn't sleep, couldn't focus in class. This is what friendship is like, she told herself. Happy friendship day, Annie!

ZEE

was thinking about how it was fine to be gay. Okay not fine, but it wasn't the end of the world. Parents came around these days. Mostly. In cities at least. In the places *they* lived. Hers pretended to be fine with it, very supportive. In fact, when she introduced Kamna as her girlfriend six months ago, her mother immediately put a rainbow sticker on her workhorse purse. It was kind of tacky but sweet at the same time.

Of course it helped that she had Didi to smooth the way. But you still had to be hot. And Annie … Annie was odd. Big nose, thick eyebrows, small mouth, eyes that were too intense. And she didn't seem to have any friends. Not really. She remembered now that time in sixth grade when everyone had to give a presentation on their aspiration, and Annie's presentation had been about how she wanted to be a nun. Who does that?

But there was something about that girl.

Obviously, she looked nothing like Kamna or any of the hotties in their grade. She did have an arresting smile, though. And what would it be like to open up her tight braids?

Annie

could hardly wait for Friday evening. At the same time she dreaded it enormously. They had agreed to meet at PVR Priya in Basant Lok market. Allegedly, it used to be the cool place to hang out back in her mother's college days as well. Imagine. It was all revamped now of course. The vegan cafe there had a chocolate Snickers cake she dreamt about sometimes. Maybe if they enjoyed the film ... they could even go have a bite there.

ZEE

was stupidly, uncharacteristically nervous on Friday. She and Annie had waved at each other briefly from opposite ends of the field but neither had crossed over that morning. She rumpled her curly hair again and again, until it sat up straight at the back of her head. 'You look like a parrot, dude. What're you doing?' Nikki said, straightening it out.

'Sorry, sorry,' she said. 'Just thinking.'

The bell rang, signalling the blessed end of the day, the school week, and almost time for her hang-out solo with Annie Gomes. 'See you at seven, haan,' her friend said.

'See you,' she said automatically. 'Wait, seven what? Where?'

'Where's your head at, Zee? Puja's tonight? Helloooo?'

'I … totally spaced. I-I have to go out with my mom,' Zee said.

'Are you serious? Puja's *not* going to be happy.'

Annie

waited at the theatre at six-thirty. She had a small bucket of popcorn in her hand. The show started at six forty-five but there were always trailers, and that PSA about Sunita who came to a dire end from smoking. She smoothed her skirt nervously, and looked at her cardigan in the big shiny gold surface of the doors. It was a small theatre. There was no way she could miss Zee.

She'd even let her hair down, like a ridiculous makeover montage in a movie. Of course she had kept her glasses on. She had to see every gory improbable death. She glanced again at the entrance. A twenty-something couple walked in, the man with sunglasses on for some reason, and his arm thrown casually, confidently across the girl's shoulders.

She looked again and her heart plummeted to her gut. It was a group of her classmates—Zee's friends, actually—traipsing in, a noisy chittering group, like babblers. They weren't afraid of attracting attention. She slunk behind into a corner, her heart beating rapidly and watched them go stand in line at the snacks counter. What was happening?

'Zee!' she heard someone yell and whipped around, catching Zee's eye in the same moment. She saw Zee take her in, and then notice her friends and go completely red.

'You came! What happened to the thing with your mother?' one of the girls was asking.

Zee stammered something quiet, and waved at the group. She stood rooted to the spot for a long moment and then, without a glance at Annie, went over to join them.

Zee

knew she had totally fucked everything up. Fuck. Fuck.

Annie

should have known better. She slunk into the theatre by herself and sat near the front in a corner. As she watched people die in inventive ways (strangled by space-heater wire, impaled by flying shark tooth, haemorrhage after being suddenly paralysed and then vacuumed by the Roomba), she mechanically ate her popcorn. She didn't register much. Her cheeks were still flaming. At least she hadn't been Carrie'd, she told herself. At least it wasn't winter formal and no one was throwing pig's blood on her.

ZEE

looked for Annie in the early mornings before practice for the next two weeks but she never showed then. She came right on time for practice and looked through Zee like they were strangers. Which they were. Then why did Zee feel so bad? Like she'd just missed a bus taking her someplace she really wanted to go. Stop this nonsense, she told herself.

At recess she couldn't help noticing that Annie hung out with some of the girls from the other section sometimes. What was her name? Rhea or something. Good for her.

ANNIE

thought Zee was probably back with Kamna. She had seen them talking at recess, and dawdling after school at the bus stop. Whatever, it didn't matter. She was doing good, actually. She maybe had two whole actual friends. And the more she ran (in secret now, in her apartment complex) the stronger she felt, the longer she could keep going. In fact, she felt more awake when she woke up in the mornings, wanted to hide less. Did ... even her face look brighter?

'Good to see you glowing, Anniepie,' her mother said that evening when they took the car out. The Nile track team was going to Lodhi Garden for one final session the evening before the big day and her mother had volunteered to drive them.

Annie found herself suddenly calm. Practice went well. In the evening, tired, happy and red-faced, they walked back with their arms around each other. They crossed aunties in sweater-kurta-sneakers doing evening-walk and round uncles importantly jogging, kids with ribbons in their hair and couples on every bench. Annie felt a surge of happiness so intense she thought her chest would burst.

'What's up with you?' asked one of the girls, Vijeta.

Annie grinned. 'Nothing, just feeling happy.'

'Yes, damn, smell that good winter smell,' Rhea said.

'It's saptaparni!' Annie was delighted to point it out. And then she was off prattling about it to her actual friends, as they walked to the Lodhi Garden gates, and waited for the naan-khatai man to pack up steaming warm biscuits. The moon was a cut golden pear hanging in the sky.

ZEE

sailed through the 400m race, winning it by a mile. She was a beautiful sight. Strong, toned calves, and legs that pumped like pistons. It was a pleasure for the audience to watch her run and she knew it. She revelled in it, letting the chants of 'Zee, Zee, Zee' fill her up. She felt the wind rush through her curls and on the back of her neck, and sped up as she saw the finish line approach. She tore through the ribbon and everyone was shouting 'Amazon, Amazon, Amazon'. Thanks to her, Amazon was in the lead. Nile was second—that girl Annie hung around with a lot, Rhea. 'Good game.' They shook hands. It was easy to be a sport when you'd won.

Soon it was the last event, the relay race. She knew Annie would be running for Nile. She went to the front lines to watch. Her friends joined her. They were all happy and excited, of course they were—she was hero of the hour, man of the match.

The coach blew her whistle and they were off: Nile, Amazon, Danube, Indus. Four runners, four batons in hand, the 400m track. They always saved the relay for last because you had to finish on a note of drama. A nail-biting finish.

Zee scanned the runners and couldn't see Annie, until finally her eyes found her—bouncing on her toes with the other closers. Wow. That's a gamble. It was a close race: Amazon and Indus were in the lead. The entire crowd was on their feet screaming the names of their houses, the runners. The field was a wall of sound.

By the second runner, Nile was last and Amazon was first. The third runner tried to make it up valiantly and got near Danube but Nile was still trailing. Zee felt awful for Annie. How humiliating. She stood there, hand outstretched, waiting for the baton, practically vibrating. She had pinned her braids, coiled up, tightly at the sides of her head. She looked like a small, big-eyed bird actually. Zee felt a twinge in her chest, and looked at her friends beside her. She stepped forward.

'Come on, Annie,' she called out, her voice shaking a bit. She clapped. 'Let's go, Annie!'

Her friends nudged her in surprise but she wasn't looking. The fourth runners of all the houses were running now, except Annie, who was waiting for the third runner from Nile to limp over to her. She didn't know if Annie heard her but she kept clapping. Amazon was still in the lead.

Finally, Annie had the baton in her hand and she was off. The crowd was roaring, an indecipherable mess of names and words and chants, at an unbearable decibel. Annie sped and sped like a machine, lighter on her feet than anyone would have thought. She passed the runner in front of her from Danube, and then incredibly, leaving the runner from Indus outraged, she crossed her too. The crowd was going nuts. Amazon was in the lead, just ten metres to go. Zee stepped out in front.

'Come on, Annie, let's fucking Go!' she shouted. And Annie, oh Annie shot forward like magic, like in slow motion, they all saw her cross the runner from Amazon, whose face fell in disbelief, and just a second before her, Annie tore through the ticker tape. All of Nile scrambled on to the field and threw themselves on top of her.

'Bloody good show,' Zee said to herself. She would have to explain to her friends but right then she didn't care. She saw Annie look at her from across the field, and she winked. 'Oh Annie you're so fine, you're so fine you blow my mind, go Annie, go go go Annie,' Nile was chanting.

ANNIE

was speechless. Finally, after many, many cheers, and accepting the trophy, and an honorary man of the match from her track team, after many sweaty hugs, and non-birthday bumps and kisses, she was packing up her bag and walking to the field. They were all going to go over to Nirula's to celebrate. Get the iconic HCF—hot chocolate fudge. She could almost taste it. Her mouth watered. And ... had that really been Zee chanting her name in public?

The stands were almost empty at this point. Someone called her name. 'Hey Annie, I want to show you something. You got a minute?'

Annie turned slowly. 'I don't know,' she said. 'I'm a champ now. My time is precious.'

'I know,' Zee said. 'As your humble fan, I want to show you something you'll like.' And she gestured towards the saptaparni tree. As they began to walk towards it, Zee took her hand, cautioning her to tread softly. A jolt of electricity went through Annie's entire body.

'Aren't you afraid someone will see?' Annie whispered.

Zee pointed up. On top of the devil's tree, sat the elusive pair of grey hornbills Annie had waited for all these mornings. Behind them the winter moon hung in the sky, full and round like a peach. The sky was pink as the sun melted into the evening.

Zee took both of Annie's hands in hers and stepped closer. 'I hope they do see,' she said. And then she kissed her.

Discord

Nisha Susan

My family can't understand my English problem. They are all very good at English. My sister could have become an English professor if she wanted but decided to study maths instead. Even my older brother, who is doing a PhD in physics and is not as smart as my sister, used to get really high marks in English. It's hard to explain doing badly in English when that's the only language you speak.

When I said I wanted to go abroad to study marine biology, my parents were like, hmm. They looked shady and wouldn't give me a straight answer. My brother Ajay didn't reply to my text for three days. He was like that even before he went to the UK. Then I got a text: 'bro, you have MIT ambitions but I am not sure even a local Bangalore college will take you with your marks.' I almost threw my phone from the balcony. What a brother. What a family.

After first term, when I brought it up again, my mother said, 'Okay, let me think about it,' and then she drove off to work. That weekend she said, 'Michael, if you really want to go to the US, we have to hire an education consultant.' Nobody said aloud what I knew they were thinking. Ajay and Aisha never needed education consultants to get into whatever university they wanted to get into. I never tell anyone what a freak Aisha is because people will think I am lying. One university in the US actually paid her plane tickets to get her to come for an interview. Actually. She flew to the US, got treated poshly, rejected them and went to Germany instead. Now Aisha has an Indian boyfriend in Australia whom she met when she was going up a mountain somewhere in Europe. Ajay *might* have a girlfriend. I don't know. It took me a long time to find out about Aisha's boyfriend, that too indirectly, and not because she told me. Because we are the only three family members in India who don't have a three-member WhatsApp group. I would never text Aisha for anything. I don't think she even remembers that she has a second brother.

The education consultant was as bad as my dentist. She looked at my class ten marks and rolled her eyes at my mother. My mother pretended to look strict and rolled her eyes at me. I sat in the black swivel chair and thought for the millionth time about what a surfboard would feel like under my chest and stomach when I first wade into the water. The light would be just perfect. I could imagine my hands in the water. One of my Fortnite friends who has lived there told me California is colder than I think. But, I know, I just *know* the sea is going to be warm, just right, just perfect, like a liquid bed. When I surfaced from the wave, my mother and the consultant lady had agreed that I would have to take coaching classes four days a week for the next year. I knew it was coming so I didn't feel bad until I realized I had to take English coaching also. On Sunday mornings. English classes. No more football.

I looked at my mother, who had clearly forgotten her plan to look strict and was looking sadly at me.

'Sundays. What about football?' I said quietly.

The consultant woman jumped up, as if I had said something terrible like, 'What about my regular Sunday morning plan of getting high on Meow Meow while wearing no clothes?'

'Young man, your English marks are so bad there is no chance, zero chance, hundred per cent zero chance that you will crack TOEFL. And what about your personal statement? Who is going to write that while you play football?'

I didn't dare look directly at her. I was afraid I might see her nose hair or spit or something gross that she produced while being angry. That *would* make me want to really get high.

My mother is really useless. Here I was arranging my face to look extra sad and repentant so we could get out of there, while she was definitely trying not to laugh at the angry consultant lady. She hustled me out of there and took me to Bangarpet Chaat. I didn't try to argue with her about missing football. She knew that in the last six years I had never missed a game except in the beginning of the pandemic. No use talking about it. If I wanted to get away from my parents and not be the last useless child at home without a life, without having any fun, then I had to sort out my marks.

I did it. No one, not my parents or Ajay or even Aisha could say I didn't try. I went to all the classes. I didn't miss one. I didn't complain. When occasionally the classes were online, I didn't miss those either. I even kept my camera on. I had so little time for gaming that Piglu cursed me regularly. The one Saturday evening I got online, Piglu got so excited he somehow convinced me to play Minecraft with him. We don't really play

Minecraft anymore. But his younger brother Nayan is really into it now. At some point we had a zombie after us. Piglu and I got away but Nayan didn't. He yelled, 'Piglu! Don't leave me. I am your brother! How can you leave me?' Piglu and I were so charged up, we didn't register his yelling for a few minutes. But he was so loud I had to take my headphones off. He was blasting my eardrums. Then Piglu started laughing at Nayan because he was doing all this dying-dying-dead-zombie-got-me drama at his brother who was sitting on the same sofa. I started laughing also but I don't know why I felt like crying at the same time thinking of Nayan being left behind in a war. Imagine someone having to make a choice like that. What if my girlfriend and I were surfing and there was a shark? What if I had to save either my girlfriend or myself? What if she had to decide whether to save herself or me?

My science and maths marks got somewhat better. My English marks were still crap. After three months, the education consultant lady sent my mother a stinker of an email. My mother was furious when she showed it to my father. My father is on my mother's side if she has a problem with anyone but him. That's how they started hanging out in engineering college—my father wanted to solve all her problems and my mother likes to keep everyone busy. My father was all ready to drive to Lavelle Road and give the consultant a kick. My mother distracted him and sent him off on a task with the residents' association before he realized that I was the one who needed to be kicked. She knew I was on the landing and could hear everything. After he left, I came downstairs and said, 'I don't know what to do.' Obviously, my mother didn't either. I just couldn't write.

A week later, my mother found a whole new coaching class for my English. Before I joined the new classes, I got one Sunday morning with football. Just one. Everyone was so happy to see me after three months, but I could see they hadn't missed me the way I had missed them. The way I had missed that muddy field and ripped-up nets and all their stupid faces. Two girls had joined—an update that no one had bothered to tell me. They were okay players even though they were tiny. One of them barely came up to my shoulders. No complaints, but no one had told me? I couldn't understand it. I felt a little bad about it the whole week.

On Saturday night, before the first new English class, I told my mother that I didn't want to go. Obviously, I was in an extra stupid mood because I said it in front of my father. My father whipped around like a cobra and said in Telugu, 'When you wanted 10,000-rupee running lessons I didn't tell you to bloody run, one leg at a time. It's free! Now you need English tuitions. Imagine telling anyone that you need English tuitions.'

I don't know how I have not broken a bottle on my father's head by now. These lessons that he is talking about happened a long time ago! Two years ago! For three months, my best friend Piglu and I had gone to these weekend classes for running. The coach over there, Ankush, made us faster permanently.

He fixed our gait, taught us all these Indian games like Kho-Kho and Lagori. It was great. Ankush was great. My father has not stopped complaining about the money. Two years later. As if he doesn't spend that kind of money when he sneezes. I hated it when he was mean to me in Telugu because I can understand it but I can't say anything back. I could feel tears of anger in my eyes so I left the room. My father yelled something again but this time I really couldn't understand what he was saying. My mother called out to me but I ignored her. The next morning, I left the house much earlier than I needed to for the English class.

On the way, I got a WhatsApp message from my mother: 'This English teacher is like Ankush. You will like her.' My mother had some serious skills. Right away I could see the new coaching class was not a regular one. The teacher, Rathi, looked normal, not impressive or good-looking like Ankush but when we did grammar, I understood it. Then we had speaking practice, which was also fine. One guy sitting next to me was on his phone most of the time. He had it hidden somehow between his lap and his desk. We were only twelve people, unlike my other classes which easily had fifty. No one was from my school, which I felt so relieved about.

Before starting the writing session, Miss Rathi said, 'I am going to tell you a secret. If you write simply, if you write your thoughts clearly, in a way that your younger brothers or sisters can understand, you will do well in TOEFL. It doesn't have to be fancy, I promise.' I saw that the guy with the phone, Riteish, had the same expression as me. He hadn't spoken once in class and was still fiddling with his phone. I looked around at the rest of the class who also looked mildly unhappy. When I saw their faces, I thought to myself, *These people must be as bad at English as I am. Awesome.* I closed my eyes and thought about floating on my back in the Pacific Ocean.

Our homework for the week was to write about a person who had a big impact on our lives. 'Just one page, only one page. It has to be meaningful. It has to be true. But just one page.' Miss Rathi smiled at all of us.

I spent the whole week feeling like vomiting. I couldn't make myself open my laptop to write but I couldn't stop thinking about the assignment either. On Wednesday, Miss Rathi sent us an email reminding us that we were supposed to write for five minutes every day so that by Friday we would have something good and not something rushed and last minute. By Friday, I felt nausea as soon as I woke up. It didn't go away the whole day. I just wanted Saturday to be over.

Dinnertime. My father was looking weirdly at me. Probably because I hadn't spoken to him in a week. I ate only three parathas and a little chicken.

My father said, 'Starving won't make you smarter.' My mother almost knocked her green tea over when she swung around to glare at him. 'Vikram.' Her voice was a warning. My father tried to look like he didn't care. He said, 'I know him. He is avoiding work. I know that face.'

I hated that my father *knew* me, even though he never cared about me or tried to understand me or helped me with my problems the way my mother did.

My mother looked at me fiercely. 'That's not true. He is working hard.' I didn't say anything, and just went to my room. After half an hour of feeling like a flattened cardboard box, I forced myself to get up. I opened my laptop and tried to start writing. *A person who had a big impact on me.*

Thirty minutes later, I hadn't written a single sentence. I hadn't even been able to think of anyone to write about. Then I saw Piglu on Discord. He asked me if I wanted to play. I said no, I had an essay to write. I didn't tell him I was in remedial English classes. He thought I had an assignment for school. 'Just use ChatGPT!' he exclaimed. 'I use it all the time.' I ignored him but Piglu kept messaging me telling me to just finish my assignment on ChatGPT and play Fortnite. I ran away from Discord. It was eleven-thirty and I wanted to sleep. What could Miss

Rathi do to me if I didn't write the essay? I got into bed.

Ten minutes later I got out of bed and signed up on ChatGPT. I told ChatGPT to write a one-page essay about Ankush, my running coach. I typed in some basic information about him, which I got from Google. Before I could blink, ChatGPT spat out an essay at me. What was this crazy speed? I started reading it and it sounded ... bad. It didn't sound like Ankush. At this point I was ready to cry and give up on everything. Even ChatGPT couldn't help me write. The stupid essay sounded like it was written by a robot about a robot. It didn't sound real. There was no way I was going to get into a US university. I was going to have to listen to my father tell every visitor that I was the only person in the family without an international degree. And according to the World's Greatest Ajay, I didn't have what it took for a local college either. I should tell my father he was right about me. But before that I had to somehow get through the coaching classes. I never wanted to hear my parents say that I failed because

I didn't go to the classes they paid for. I just had to make it to the end of the year when coaching classes ended. I took many deep breaths and tried to get my act together.

ChatGPT couldn't write about anyone real but maybe it could help me get me through tomorrow's class. I tried hard to focus. I wish I had a girlfriend I could text instead of Piglu. Where would I meet my girlfriend? At the beach, I thought. I had barely been to the ocean a dozen times in my life but I knew it would change my life. If I got to the beach I could find a girlfriend. Why was I born into a family that lived in Bangalore? If I lived on the coast, I would meet someone like Patricia Ornelas.

Patricia Ornelas is a lady surfer who lives in Mexico. She is the GOAT, in my opinion. She sometimes wears funny outfits when surfing, like a skirt. One time she wore a bodysuit with a skeleton print and flowers in her hair for Mexican Halloween. That's not why I liked her. I liked her because she surfed like she was just taking a walk, just strolling on the waves. Casual like. No effort. I had seen a hundred videos on Insta and she was smiling in all of them. Not showing all her teeth but just smiling and walking on water.

What if I met my girlfriend Patricia the surfer for the first time when I was surfing at sunrise? I asked ChatGPT. ChatGPT spat out a story again at me. A whole story about how I met her. I read it. It sounded ... great, I thought! I changed some things that ChatGPT had cooked up. Changed Mexico to Mangalore and all. Then I changed the story a little. In ChatGPT's version of how I met my girlfriend we were too grown-up-sounding. I had to tell the app that we were sixteen. I did tell the app that when I first met Patricia she was wearing her skeleton suit and flowers in her hair. And that she really liked Chicken Ghee Roast and sweet-and-salty mix fresh lime soda. And that she didn't like to dance at all but she was a great swimmer.

Whatever. At least I had something to take to class tomorrow. I uploaded the assignment and then I was so relieved, I went to sleep right away. I dreamt that an octopus had come to dinner and eaten all my parathas.

I was so relaxed the next morning in class. A couple of people read their essays before me. One was pretty bad. One was okay. Miss Rathi made us give our feedback after each person read, which ordinarily would have made me run out of the room. But that morning I had played football. The Sunday game had been moved half an hour earlier than usual so I could actually play before class. One of the two girls had said she had coaching classes on Sunday so everyone agreed to prepone it. Why hadn't *I* asked? Anyway, we had a great game and I was feeling so loose muscled in class that I actually raised my hand to give feedback to someone else's essay.

When it was my turn, I made sure I read slowly and clearly. In school, there was no chance that I would ever, ever, ever write about a girlfriend in an essay. Or read it out. Never. I knew somehow that Miss Rathi would be cool. She looked at me sharply a couple of times while I was reading out the piece but when

I finished, she didn't say anything. She looked around at the class and said, 'Well, what feedback do we have for Michael?' Everyone was silent for a bit but then one girl raised her hand. This was the girl with many, many stickers on her laptop. 'I thought it was beautiful. Really beautiful.'

'Yeah, beautiful!' said the guy with the blue glasses.

I felt funny in my chest. I looked at Miss Rathi. She had no expression on her face but I felt like she might be smiling. She asked the class, 'What did you find beautiful?'

The first girl said, 'The words to describe the girl, the waves, the light behind her.'

'The light?' asked Miss Rathi.

Another guy raised his hand. 'The description of the light at the beach was great. Is this a true story?'

I said, 'Yes.' It was true enough, I thought. But I had barely a second to think because the guy who asked the question said, 'Well done, man!' and everyone laughed, including Miss Rathi.

More smiling, happy feedback. Miss Rathi asked people to think and say sensible things instead of saying 'Beautiful, beautiful'. 'Which sentence did you like, what did you think about the dead jellyfish that Michael spotted on the beach?' Everyone said interesting things except for Riteish, who was sitting next to me. Like the previous week, he didn't speak at all and was fiddling with his phone. Miss Rathi must have spotted him as well because she asked him directly what he thought. To my surprise he said something intelligent-sounding. I could see Miss Rathi also looked surprised. I was pretty sure he hadn't written his assignment. Because it wasn't open on his laptop.

During our five-minute break many people complimented me. The girl with the stickered laptop asked me, 'So your girlfriend is in Mangalore?'

I said 'Yes' and ran to the bathroom.

After the break, Rathi said we had run out of reading time. Now we had to improve our essays. Really think about how to say directly that this is how the person we wrote about changed our lives. And also check all the grammar and spelling mistakes.

I flexed sideways because I had a bit of pain in my bum where I had fallen on a stone in the field that morning and suddenly I could see what Riteish was doing. He had ChatGPT open on his phone. He must have been using ChatGPT to give feedback on everyone's essays. What a useless fellow! And here I was wondering how come he was giving feedback using such fancy English. Riteish looked up and saw my disgusted face. His eyes had subtitles: like, *what's your problem?* Then I remembered that I had also used ChatGPT. I felt like an old birthday balloon. I stared at my screen. I closed my eyes. I had to get through this year somehow. And maybe I would pass TOEFL or maybe I wouldn't. And I would figure something. I had figured football. Sort of.

Miss Rathi came up to my row. First, she sat down next to Riteish and spoke very quietly to him. He looked sheepish and was wriggling on his bum. Had she figured that he was using ChatGPT? Had she figured I was too?

She got up from the chair next to Riteish and came up to me. 'That was an unexpected piece of writing, Michael. I enjoyed it,' she said. I didn't know what to do with my face.

Miss Rathi said, 'I want you to think hard now and think about what Patricia means. More than a girlfriend. Why is she the person who has changed your life? It's not because of her skeleton suit, was it?' She was smiling as she looked down at me. I looked at her face and thought that she probably woke up feeling like she could walk on water anytime she wanted. No one would make her feel like an NPC. She said, 'Okay, get started on the thinking. The writing will follow.'

I got started on the writing. How had Patricia changed my life? Well, she loved the ocean like me and she understood why I wanted to become a marine biologist. Patricia also surfed every day. If I could, I would have played football every day. She knew that you had to do it first thing every day. She understood that even if your parents came from a place in Andhra far from the coast and lived in Bangalore, you could see the ocean just a few times in your life and know that you belonged on the beach with a surfboard and a sweet dog. Patricia of Mexico. Patricia who lived inside ChatGPT. And in the light of a sunrise in Mangalore.

After class, outside the building, the girl with the stickered laptop smiled at me before leaving. Riteish came up to me. He stood a little too close. He had very thick eyelashes and a little bit of a baby face even though he was taller than me. He said, 'Good luck with your girlfriend.' He sounded like he meant it.

Accidentally Enemies

Andaleeb Wajid

Planning a vacation with three families should have been a nightmare for the adults who had to figure out the logistics and god knows what else. But this time, it was a nightmare for two of the young adults who were travelling with this group of noisy, nosy and chatty people.

There was no time for either of the young adults to dissect this matter to death with their respective friends before they got on to the minivan that was going to take them to Ooty. Ahad's mother, Sanobar, had been running around like a headless chicken for three days before the actual trip. So much so that Ahad's father, Maqdoom, had considered calling off the trip altogether. But he'd already paid for the minivan and booked their cottage in Ooty, so he decided that Sanobar's theatrics could be tolerated for a little longer.

Ahad had felt a brief moment of hope when his father threatened to cancel the trip. But then Abba informed them that they had better help their mother and do whatever she wanted them to do so she didn't stress so much. This meant ferrying empty suitcases to Areesha's house and lugging back the dabbas of food that Areesha's mother, Huma Aunty, would give him because their fridge was bigger. Suffice to say, the lift between his house and Areesha's worked overtime during this period.

He tried to palm off these jobs to Ayman, his younger sister, because she was Areesha's best friend but Ammi didn't want to send Ayman for this very reason.

'Those two will not get any work done! They'll be jabbering all the time,' Ammi told him. He stared at her unironically, considering that was exactly what she did whenever she holed up with Areesha's mother.

Ahad really wanted to punch the person who had come up with the idea of a combined family trip to Ooty, considering that Areesha hated the sight of him. *And with good reason,* he thought glumly. He'd ruined everything between them before it could even begin.

No one really slept the night before the trip, mostly because the three fathers (Ahad's, Areesha's and her cousin Iqra's) were constantly going up and down the floors of Starville Apartments, where they all lived, bringing down suitcases, remembering that they'd forgotten to pack sweaters and so on. The building was his father's but he'd sold flats to his friends and their relatives, and sometimes it was all so much like a sickeningly sweet *Hum Aapke Hain Kaun* montage that it made him nauseous.

Way before the Fajr azaan even sounded in the masjid nearby, the fathers had assembled everyone downstairs. It was half past four. The roads were dark. In the distance, they could hear a few cars but there wouldn't be much traffic. The mothers were huddled in their shawls, as if they were already in Ooty, instead of regular old Bangalore.

Since Ahad and Yasir, Areesha's brother, were the only teenage boys in the group, all the heavy work fell to them. Ahad really wished his friend Kamran could have come along with them but Kamran's father was very strict and would have never given him permission.

The thing was that Yasir was a bit scary. He was a little older than Ahad but he was already taller and way more muscly. And then there was the issue of Areesha hating him now and she'd obviously told her brother why. Yasir glowered at him as the two of them loaded the suitcases in the back of the minivan. Ahad had tried to joke about the amount of food they were taking, as if they were going somewhere without restaurants, and Yasir had scowled at him. So Ahad had given up talking to him, even more so when Yasir cornered him as he was taking the cooler full of juice cartons to the minivan.

'If I see you near my sister, I'll beat you to a pulp and wipe my shoes on you,' he growled as he walked away.

'Rude,' Ahad muttered, but he also shuddered, aware that Yasir could very well carry out his threat.

Just when everything was loaded, the first Fajr azaan sounded out and the fathers wouldn't leave until they'd prayed. Areesha's father, Gulzar Uncle, insisted they all go to his house where the men could pray together in the living room and the women could do the same in one of the other rooms.

Naturally, after this, Sarfaraz Uncle asked if it was possible to get a cup of tea. And then Iqra's mother,

Nehmat Aunty, remembered that she had forgotten something important and she wanted to go and get it. They lived on the top-most floor and before Huma Aunty could stop her, she'd already left.

This meant that by the time they all got into the minivan, it was nearly seven.

Ahad was sitting up in front, feeling miserable about this weekend trip all over again. He could have been playing cricket with Kamran and Vishal. He could have gone to watch *Avengers* with them. He could have done so much more instead of being saddled with his very *extra* family.

All his thoughts ground to a halt when he saw her. Their eyes connected and held. Areesha looked fresh-faced and pink, and she'd tied her hair in a ponytail that made it look slinky and did all kinds of things to his insides. She was wearing jeans and a longish green top, and a white scarf was slung casually around her neck. She looked cool and elegant. Her nostrils flared ever so briefly before she walked towards the back of the minivan. Ayman came next and she made a face at him as she followed Areesha. Great. Of course his sister would take Areesha's side.

His older sister, Tazeen Apa, came up next. She looked around for a place to sit and finally settled near one of the windows and pushed the curtain aside. Iqra, who was a little younger than all of them, came next, her eyes scanning the minivan for Ayman and Areesha. Ahad was aware of how the girls tried to avoid Iqra because she was so talkative.

'They're at the back,' he mouthed deviously. Iqra happily gave him a two-finger salute as she sashayed towards them in her lurid pink salwar kameez. God, if he stared at her for too long, he was likely to get a migraine.

Finally, everyone was seated and the minivan started the long, interminable journey to Ooty.

Suddenly, his phone pinged. He looked down at the screen. Abba had bought him a phone only recently. At least he had this, he thought as he checked the message.

It was from Kamran. *How's chammak challo?*

* * *

'It's been nearly a year now?' Ayman asked in a hushed whisper as she settled deeper into her seat.

Areesha exhaled, her breath condensing on the glass window. Absently, she drew a heart and the letters A and A inside it. Then she had a sickening realization of what she'd done, and she quickly ran her palm over it, obliterating the heart and the letters.

Areesha and Ahad.

She'd been so silly, so foolish. She turned to her best friend, who also happened to be her enemy's sister.

'I'm not keeping track,' she lied. It had been ten months actually, since she'd heard Ahad and his friends braying over that shitty poem he'd written about her in the stairwell of Starville Apartments.

'I know he's a horrible, horrible, disgusting ass,' Ayman said fervently. 'But he's not that bad a human being.'

Areesha gave her a long look. 'Really?'

Ayman sighed. 'Okay fine.'

Areesha's face heated. She felt her scalp prickle at the memory of that infamous poem. She and Ahad had grown up together in Starville Apartments, had been part of many combined games, dumb charades and Pictionary championships, often on opposing sides, but for the past couple of years, there had been something different about the way he looked at her. It made her feel all sorts of things inside and she didn't quite know what to make of it. Then there were a few times when they'd been paired together in the games and they were almost always in sync, so much so that Yasir had claimed they were cheating. It gave her a sort of thrill to think about those moments. And that's why she'd started looking at him differently too.

There was also the fact that he'd become tall, lean and really, *really* cute.

Once, a friend from school, Nazish, had come home and they were both standing on the balcony when

Nazish asked her who the hot guy playing basketball was. *Hot guy? Indeed.* She'd felt shy and somewhat hopeful that maybe something could happen between them.

But then the awful poem incident happened, the words of which were now seared into her memory—

Chalti hai woh kamar matak matak ke,

gir jaate hain uske chaahne waale patak patak ke

Uske bhainse jaisi chaal,

uske joker jaise gaal,

uske chamkadar jaise baal ...

She sat up straight and shook her head. 'I can't decide if he's a terrible human being or a terrible poet.'

Ayman sighed dramatically. 'I was kind of hoping that you two would, you know ...' She blushed. Areesha shot her a look just as the bus lurched forward. Her stomach twisted and she felt the slightest bit nauseous.

'The two of us would ...?' she asked.

'Get together,' Ayman said in a hushed whisper, indicating the seat ahead of them. Nosy Iqra was sitting there. They couldn't escape her anywhere. The problem with having her around was that she talked a lot and didn't let anyone else say anything. And the moment someone did say something, there was a hundred per cent chance that the elders would hear about it soon enough. Areesha had confronted her once about being a tattle-tale and Iqra had been tearfully defensive, saying that she just liked to talk. She just didn't realize whom she was talking to, until it was quite late.

Areesha made a face. Get together with that no-good, useless Ahad? Never. Even if he'd grown annoyingly cuter in the months since that poem … not that she'd looked at him properly or anything! But she thought of the way he'd looked at her right now as she got on the minivan and felt a burst of pleasure at the way his eyes had widened in appreciation.

Of *course* she hadn't dressed for his benefit. Of *course* she hadn't worn her long, silky hair in a sleek ponytail to swish it around enticingly. Of *course* she hadn't dabbed her face twice with a compact to make sure her face wasn't shiny. In the days after that humiliating poem, she had cried to Nazish and Ayman, feeling all her insecurities about herself rise up. Both of them had been livid on her behalf. She'd found it was easier to talk about Ahad to Nazish though, and one day when Ayman hadn't come over, Nazish had told her that maybe Ahad liked her despite the poem.

'Whose side are you on? Mine or his?' she asked.

'Always yours. But I've noticed the way he looks at you when you walk past him in the building,' Nazish said hesitantly.

'What do you mean?' Areesha's heart pounded the slightest bit.

'There's definitely something there,' Nazish said firmly.

'Yeah, he's probably looking for more things to write poems about and humiliate me.'

But Nazish had been doubtful and she'd sowed that seed in Areesha. So instead of lifting her nose in the air the next time she saw him, she glanced at him once or twice and noted that her friend was right.

But that didn't make what he'd done okay. Maybe he was still attracted to her. Maybe boys like him were really into chamkadar jaise baal. Who knew?

'We're not. We won't,' she said firmly. Ayman sighed and folded her arms across her chest but she didn't push it. She knew when to let things be, which was why she was her best friend. Too bad she had such a loser for a brother.

The aunties were chattering away in the middle row while the uncles guffawed, but Areesha's eyes kept getting drawn to the head of hair she knew was Ahad's. She stared at the back of his neck for long moments and then looked away, feeling idiotic. She'd sooner replace his shampoo with hair-removing cream than get together with him.

When they stopped on the outskirts of Mandya for breakfast, Areesha felt the first stirrings of unease. When they had got on the van, she had been too busy trying to ignore Ahad and she'd been sitting by the window, letting the cool air wash over her. She disliked road trips as a rule because she got car sick but her mother had been so excited about this one that Abba had thought nothing of agreeing to Ahad's father's invitation. He thought they would all be happy about it. She really hoped she'd be spared of any vomiting incidents in the van. She'd never be able to live it down.

Areesha avoided looking at Ahad, who was being super helpful to her parents, making sure Ammi had a nice seat on the bench. They'd stopped somewhere scenic and the women unpacked the food they'd made. Areesha frowned when she saw the amount of food they'd all packed.

She examined her samosa and then made a face.

'What? It's kheema samosa! I know it's your favourite,' Iqra said. 'Ammi woke up at three in the morning to fry them.'

Areesha shook her head. Her mother had been awake at some absurd hour as well, the fragrance of onions and adrak lehsun for the biryani that they'd be having for lunch later that day permeating the air.

'This is so weird. If it's a vacation, why are our mothers working harder than ever?' she mused. 'There are so many restaurants along the highway. Why can't we just stop somewhere and eat?'

'Because it would be expensive?' Iqra said. Areesha rolled her eyes.

'Nothing beats homemade food for them,' Ayman added with a shrug.

Areesha stiffened when she noticed Ahad coming over with a juice box in his hand. He'd better not be bringing it to her like some sort of peace offering. He'd better not act like nothing had happened. The thoughts streamed through her head like a ticker tape that came to a halt when Ahad stopped before her. And then he handed the juice box to Iqra, who took it from him with a smile.

'Thanks, Ahad bhai!' she said.

'No problem,' he said, but this time, he was looking at Areesha. She felt her face heat and her belly flip at his nearness, but she pushed the feeling away as she sauntered towards the minivan.

Post breakfast, most people dozed off. Areesha was sleepy too. That is, until they reached the hairpin bends.

***

Ahad woke up to the sound of loud retching. He shifted in his seat and turned around to the back of the van. Areesha was heaving into a plastic bag and her mother was holding back her hair by that same sleek ponytail.

Ahad turned back around swiftly. He felt bile rise in his throat and he shut his eyes tightly. Quickly shoving his earphones into his ears, he desperately picked the first song in his playlist. Any song would do. His stomach was doing all sorts of cartwheels, and if it didn't stop soon, he'd start puking too.

When the van stopped, he opened his eyes and pulled out his earphones. The music squawked, the tinny sound feeling quite loud in the silence of the van. What happened? Had they stopped the van to let her vomit in peace? He turned around and saw Huma Aunty wiping Areesha's brow. Areesha shot him a look of such hate that he turned back around instantly.

She was being mean to him for far too long now. Okay, fine, he'd been an ass. But he'd been goaded by his friends who thought he was too pansy because he liked to write poetry. They thought that growing up in a household filled with women had made him overly sensitive. And that Vishal had mocked him saying that soon his mother would tie his hair in two ponytails like Shahrukh Khan in the 'Bicchu' song in *Chamatkar*. That had been the last straw.

It was not a moment he was proud of and he acknowledged it now. Although at that time, seeing his friends chortle and slap their thighs as he recited the poem in the stairwell had made him feel ten feet tall. Until he'd found out that she had overheard *everything*.

But couldn't she let it go already? How long was she going to hold the grudge for? He'd already apologized to her several times and each time she behaved like he didn't exist, or if he did, he was the dirt under her shoe.

'Come on, we're here,' Abba said. Oh, they'd reached. Thank goodness. Before he could get out of his seat, Areesha walked past him on wobbly legs. When she saw him, she altered her posture, straightening up. So she thought she was some queen, he thought, annoyed. She was ...

'Ulti rani,' he whispered. Unfortunately for him, she heard that too and shot him a deathly glare.

Sighing, Ahad got down from the van and helped Yasir unload the luggage at the hotel's reception. Everyone was tired and achy and sleepy but the mothers were clearly made of some other stuff. They gathered everyone around briskly and informed them that lunch would be at Huma Aunty's cottage.

Ahad groaned internally as he followed his family to their cottage. He was not looking forward to seeing Areesha so soon again. But they were going to be in each other's faces all the time this weekend. Just perfect.

* * *

'I'm ulti rani is it?' Areesha muttered to herself as she freshened up in the bathroom. She was cold and miserable, and she hated it here already. She'd brushed her teeth twice and still she didn't feel good.

She walked outside and Ammi was immediately by her side. 'Kaisa hai mera baccha?' she asked. Areesha hugged her mother, feeling better instantly. She wanted to tell her mother she'd be the happiest if she didn't have to see Ahad ever again. But she knew it wasn't true and the bigger issue would be trying to explain to Ammi what had happened.

'I'm okay,' she said.

'Good. Come and help me set the table then,' Ammi said. Areesha groaned.

'Why do we have to turn even the vacation cottage into a home?' she asked.

'Stop whining. Be glad Ammi made biryani for lunch today,' Yasir muttered as he handed Ammi a microwave-safe dish. The kitchenette in the cottage had probably never seen this much action, Areesha groused but half an hour later, as they all sat around the table, inhaling Ammi's mutton biryani balanced precariously on paper plates, she had to admit it was rather nice …

… until she lifted her head and locked eyes with Ahad. Ulti rani, he mouthed to her. She felt her back turn cold, then hot, and then she knew she couldn't let this go.

Operation Annihilate Ahad was going to be put into action.

As soon as she ate her biryani.

* * *

If the only way Areesha was going to look at him was when he teased her, then that's what he was going to do, Ahad decided rather foolishly. So it was rather unfortunate that when they were all getting ready to go sightseeing, he found a huge hole in the crotch of his jeans. What the ...

He shucked it off and quickly rifled through his luggage. Ammi had been after him to pack properly but with the over confidence one can only find in seventeen-year-old boys, he had declared that he could easily survive the weekend in one pair of jeans, the ones he'd worn on the van. He'd changed into track pants for lunch and they'd all taken a quick nap before deciding to assemble for sightseeing later in the day.

Grimly, he pulled on his track pants (the *only* pair of track pants he'd brought along), and his woollen jumper and hurried outside.

It was only when he sat down in the van that he felt something odd. There was something poking his underarms. He tried to tug it away from his body but the sleeves seemed tighter than normal. He'd noticed it when he wore his jumper, but he attributed it to the muscles he was building then. Something was definitely wrong. Before he could say anything, Abba had directed the van driver to get going.

'Why are you fidgeting so much?' Ammi asked, staring at him. He kept tugging and tugging until something ripped. To his horror, he saw that his sleeve was no longer attached to his jumper.

'Did you just *tear* your sweater?' Ammi asked, looking at him in shock.

'No … I …' He heard a giggle at the back of the van—that's when he realized who was behind this. Had she also managed to make that hole in his jeans? He swivelled on the other side to glare at Ayman. It must have been her. Areesha had obviously recruited Ayman (his own sister!) to sabotage his outfits. But Ayman just looked back at him innocently, as if she had no idea what had just happened.

Ahad had no idea that it was just the beginning.

Over the weekend, Ahad encountered:

1. A too-salty nimbu pani

2. Gobi Manchurian with too generous a helping of green chillies that made his eyes water like the Niagara Falls.

3. A mix of egg and water instead of his own shampoo, so when he washed his hair with hot water, he ended up with scrambled eggs on his head.

He bore it all quietly, thinking of ways to get back at Areesha. Ayman swore to him that she had nothing to do with any of those things. Although she kept wrinkling her nose as she talked because of how badly he stank of eggs.

Furious, he typed out a message to Kamran, telling him about all that had happened to him. But he paused just before hitting the send button.

Come to think of it, some of this mess was because of Kamran, who thought calling Areesha 'chammak challo' would be funny. 'She should be so honoured,' Kamran had said when Ahad asked him to cut it out. Kamran had egged him on constantly, and the result was that Poem.

Ahad's finger still hovered over the button.

Kamran would definitely help him with payback. But …

Ahad glanced over at Areesha as she sat around the bonfire that the hotel employees had made for them. Her skin glowed in the light of the fire. She looked almost ethereal. His heart gave a painful twist and he rubbed his chest. Yup, he'd totally ruined everything between them.

She caught his look and lifted her chin to show just a hint of a challenge. There were many things he wanted to do then. Walk up to her, yank her up from that chair, hold her face, kiss her.

Blinking, he reeled back a little in shock even as he knew that he had to reclaim this moment before he did something stupid. So, carefully, he rubbed his eyebrow with his middle finger, delightedly watching her face contort in anger.

But as he went to sleep that night, he thought of how badly he still wanted to kiss her.

* * *

Areesha was dreading the return trip to Bangalore. The vacation had turned out to be a lot of fun with Operation Annihilate Ahad. Oooh, he was probably ruing the day he decided to mess with her. She had more plans for him once they returned home. After all, they lived in the same building and there was a lot more that she could do to him.

Ayman's disapproval notwithstanding, Areesha made plans as they finished packing their clothes. Ahad had discarded his destroyed pullover and Sanobar Aunty had bought him a chunky yellow sweater from the market (that he'd looked at in horror when she insisted he wear it).

'He looks like Big Bird, no?' Areesha said to Ayman with a grin. Ayman rolled her eyes. Sighing, Areesha remembered that she had to get through the hairpin bends without vomiting.

'Here,' Ayman said, handing her a strip of medicine. 'Hopefully this will help.'

'Thanks!' Areesha said, hugging her instinctively. 'You're the best.'

'Actually,' Ayman said hesitantly, 'Ahad got it for you.'

Areesha froze and handed it back to her but Ayman was having none of it. 'No, please. Take it. Stop being silly. You've done enough, haven't you?'

A sudden wave of guilt washed over Areesha. Maybe she *had* gone a little overboard. She shouldn't have layered his hotel bed with onion peels that she'd collected from the restaurant kitchen, for one. But how could she forgive him so easily? How could she just move on as if nothing had happened?

Maybe she needed to learn to take the high road, she decided. After all, he'd made the first overture, by getting her this medicine. Maybe ... just maybe ... he was genuinely sorry. Well, as long as he didn't call her ulti rani again, she decided with a sniff.

The trip back home was uneventful, and Areesha tried not to make it evident that she was stealing glances at Ahad, taking in the way he looked. He somehow made that Big Bird yellow sweater work, but he pulled it off once they neared Bangalore. He'd gotten to his feet and yanked it off in a rather smooth move, which made Areesha's eyes widen in shock because he'd ended up pulling off his T-shirt too.

He caught her staring at him, and his face flushed. The aunties were asleep, as were the uncles. It felt like it was just the two of them in the minivan. She didn't look away and neither did he.

'Ahad!' Tazeen Apa said, looking at him disapprovingly. 'Wear your T-shirt. Stop showing off.'

'Who's showing off?' Yasir asked, rolling up his sleeves and glaring at Ahad. Ahad made a face and slipped his T-shirt back over his head.

Areesha decided that maybe she'd punished him enough. By the time they reached Bangalore, it was late evening. Everyone was tired and hungry, but the aunties still had it in them to make plans for dinner.

God, all they did was cook and make plans to cook, Areesha thought irritably.

But she felt a surge of anticipation inside her. Something had changed in the moment they had looked at each other in the bus. She was going to smile at Ahad when she saw him. That would be his indication that she'd let bygones be bygones. Ahad and Yasir were already unloading all the luggage. She lingered near the gate of the apartment, wondering how she would tell him that she'd forgiven him when she saw him stare open-mouthed at someone.

A girl emerged from the shadows of the stairwell, and it was Areesha's turn to stare. She had glossy shampoo commercial hair that swished around hypnotically as she walked and she was ... unbelievably pretty. Areesha felt dowdy next to her.

'That's Sana,' Iqra said, coming up behind her.

'Sana who?' Ayman asked.

'Her family's just moved to Starville. Oh look! Ahad bhai seems quite smitten, no?' she said.

Areesha didn't know how to react. Her heart felt like someone was squeezing it with a fist. When Ahad turned to say something to his father, who was paying the minivan driver, Areesha could swear she could see cartoon hearts in his eyes.

For a moment, their eyes connected.

Wait, she wanted to tell him. *I changed my mind about us. There can be an us.*

But Ahad turned to Sana and smiled at her, that full, open smile that always made her heart feel lighter. The smile that was meant for *her*. It was now directed at this Sana.

Too bad, she thought angrily, trying to mask her heartbreak as fury.

Operation Annihilate Ahad was back on, she decided as she stomped away inside the building.

She didn't see him look away from Sana.

She didn't see him look at her regretfully.

She didn't see him lift his hand and open his mouth to call out to her and drop his hand because she'd already disappeared.

The only thing she saw when she turned around just before she got into the lift was Ahad saying something softly to Sana and her trilling laughter as she got the joke.

Her eyes smarted. She was going to make sure *he* was the joke.

I'll Wait

Words and photograph by ANURAG BANERJEE

I'll wait for that night we stayed up laughing and talking and singing and dancing like we were the only people in this world, like we were the only people in this city full of people.

That night when we made vacuous promises to each other about the places we would travel to and the people we would have dinner with. That night when we spilled our secrets in different parts of the city for strangers to pick up and pass on to more strangers so that our lives would be lived more than once. When we took the cheapest mode of transport to that cheap bar and had cheap drinks and revelled in the richness of the night.

That night when you wore the colours of the night, draped it like a shawl over your shoulders and slipped your hand into mine like you were putting on a glove.

I'll wait for that night again,

I'll wait for your touch.

'Love in Bombay' is a secret about a secret; one that has no space to dwell indoors and has thus spilt out into the city.

This photograph is part of the series.

@ the party

Jerry Pinto

In the morning, I added: They would smell of cinnamon and bitter wormwood.

I don't know how bitter wormwood smells but I bet it would be perfect. I read somewhere that bitter wormwood was used in absinthe and just the name gives me goosebumps. It seems like the essence of Parisian sophistication and if you're living in Vile Parle

East, you know how much you need La Rive Gauche to manifest in your life.

Meanwhile, I make do with K-pop stars. And Édith Piaf when I am down.

The thing is: I'm non-binary. I don't know how I know but I know. I think everyone else knows too because no one wants to talk to me. The girls find me too boyish—I love contact sports. The boys find me too girlie—I love silk and I like wearing colours, bling colours, psychedelic colours. 'Padam, padam, padam ...'

My parents? They're cool with it. When I told them, they threw the classic cool shit at me: 'We love you, anyway.'

Actually, when I was diagnosed with retinitis pigmentosa, I should have been the one to say that: 'Thanks for this genetic shit you thrust on me. But I love you anyway.'

Then Flip actually said something honest. He said, 'I thought you were gay.'

And this man teaches anthropology? Boggles the mind.

Gay would be easy. Straight would be easier. If only I could believe these things exist. Where I'm standing, they're invented boxes and the boxes are built of a lack of imagination, an egotistical desire to clone oneself and the teachings of society. I can see you shaking your head. Let it go. That's what I think. You go think your think. I got no problem with your think so please let me have my think to myself, yeah?

So I was saying, my 'rents are both teachers so we're sad middle-class, means: enough money to think about vacations abroad but not enough to buy the tickets and the hotel rooms so we go abroad to places where we have relatives and can sleep on their couches and strain their patience. That kind of sad middle-class. No absinthe for our elevenses.

Flip is head of the anthropology department and Cynthia, professor of botany. They aren't spectacularly gifted to have got to these positions. Just old. I came along when they should have been eyeing my elder brother and sister for babies to make them grandkids. I mean Jonathon and Russell are in their late twenties and they should start reproducing now when the getting is good. Wait too long and then let your 'nads surprise you and you might end up with flawed goods. Like me.

I mean: how much worse does it get? A non-binary kid with retinitis pigmentosa? Skipped the first three children …

Sorry, I should tell you that their first try was a disaster.

Anthro plus Botany = Athena.

She lasted three days. She was very premature but they thought she had a fighting chance. She didn't. They still celebrate her Coming Day. They have a party for all their friends and don't tell anyone what it's about. Only they know. It gives them a thrill, I think, to be all *paaa–a–arty-time!* when they're thinking about Athena. On her Going Day, they stay at home and curl up together and cry. I don't want to tell them that this is so self-pitying and they got three more children after her and two of them at least would make most binaries proud.

As for me, they are very proud of me. They are so proud of me that I know that they can't possibly be proud of me. Look at who I am. I am a minority in this country. I am non-binary which makes me even more of a minority. I am nearly blind. I want to be a poet and let me tell you there is no money in that. I like to try and complicate things further by saying: I shall only love someone who is also a Christian non-binary near-blind person.

Tell the truth non-binary person. Tell me who you are.

Truth is: I'd love anybody who'd love me.

Truth is: I don't know if I can love because I've made irony into my handmaiden and my shield.

Truth is: I wouldn't love anybody who had the bad taste to love me.

Truth is: I'm Groucho Marx minus the eyebrows and the moustache.

And now it's prom night and I don't want to go. I dance pretty well but no one will ask me. I don't want to ask because it would be a pity yes. I don't want pity. I don't want to be danced with because you get a golden tick in your book for dancing with the near-blind incel non-binary. I want to be wanted. I want to exchange body fluids. Passionately. Under the uncaring moon whose only business seems to be to drive us mad by pulling our blood tides out of sync with reality.

Moon-mad, I shall dance.
Will you dance with me, sun?
We could be stars, you and I

Only, everyone out there is all about planets, about Mars and Venus. If that's where men and women are, well call me saturnine, see if I care.

I want so much to dance. I want so much to let my body graze their body, I want so much to let my body say what my eyes can't ...

You know that's the problem sometimes? I have dark glasses on. I wear them because I don't want to be seen staring past people when I am talking to them. I don't want people to see something, what? I don't know what, something that tells them that kid is going to be blind. I want to retreat behind black glass but how am I supposed to smoulder at them when they turn up? How am I supposed to pass the message: I want you, I love you, I need you, come hold me, without eyes? Do you know how much work the eyes do in these matters?

And then I will be sitting there and those idiots will be moving to 'YMCA' because they know the moves. May the heavens open and burst down fire on those who play 'YMCA'. Or the 'Macarena'. That's not dancing. That's exercise.

Dancing is what I do when I put on 'Chk Chk Boom' and I let myself go. I don't know the moves. I know. The moves aren't just the moves, they are the MOVES. like THE MOVES. They are carved on granite and if you don't do them, you're a dweeb. But I am so out here, so far out here, so far out in this space of minoritynonbinarydisabled that I don't give a rat's testicle what anyone thinks of my dancing.

Because I think, like, it was all white, right? I mean it was black too but it was white, even the black came through the white and it came here and we danced to it. Michael Jackson, God, think of that, was he non-binary? I think about what he did to his nose and I wonder whether he did it to be white? And his skin? Did he have vitiligo? Those boys in the bedroom? What's up with that, Mike? Only when the music plays, I forgive.

But it was all white and then K-pop made it go another way. Now if that other way is going to be oh-you-must-know-the-steps, then shuck that fit. I won't be dancing in the way they are dancing. I will be dancing the way my feet say: Be dancing @

By the way, that's my name: @

In class I go by my given name. I won't tell you what it is. It was the name that Flip and Sin gave me when they had to give me a name.

'Why did you name me that?' I asked Sin once. She was trying her hand at domesticity, cooking up a Sunday stew. This stage involved slicing onions.

Or dicing them. Or making them into a right old mess because 'It all goes into the stomach, right?'

'We had to. It's the law. But you can change it as soon as you get to eighteen. Or twenty-one. Or when you earn your first million dollars.'

'What?'

She turned her cool eyes on me.

'If you hate your name so much, you will find out, won't you?'

Flip came in and said, 'You have a perfectly nice name.'

I thought, 'You chose it so you would think it nice, wouldn't you?'

Anyway, where's @?

@ will not be @theprom #stupidkidsparty #heartbreakcity #whocateredthis #ifyoudidn't getanyyou'llendupamillionairebecausenoonewants anerd@theprom.

(I take it you get the pun?)

The next thing I know I'm in the car and Flip and Sin are both driving me to the prom. I won't take you through the whole day and the tears—not mine, Sin's—that got me into lemon silk with gold tassels and my rhinestone-studded jeans.

The prom was the usual shit. It was wafers rapidly softening, samosas rapidly cooling, limbu soda rapidly warming and a DJ who thought he was at a mixer called Autumn Leaves for senior citizens who wanted a second chance at lehrve. Tina Turner? Even Sin would have had to be dancing ironically.

Flip and Sin wanted to hang around but I said I would be fine and I would head off to my friends. I walked bravely into the gym and went up to someone, anyone, and pretended to be talking. Mera bad luck hi kharaab tha for it turned out to be Miss Binary herself, Shruti Bagdogra.

I had taken down the Shrew in a class debate about euthanasia. Actually she had taken herself down when she got really hot and bothered and said, 'Well, if I were your parents, I would give you a lethal injection.'

That got her into some serious shit. Since then she hasn't spoken to me. Ever.

'It's you!' she said. 'Please go away ...'

'Just until my parents leave,' I said.

'Okay,' she said but I was aware that my parents were still watching so I pretended to be all excited and flapped my arms up and down and pretended to be super-excited. I didn't know how to semaphore happiness across the space but I heard Flip say, 'I think he's okay' and Sin say, 'I think *they're* okay' in a will-you-never-get-it tone. Poor Flip, he still isn't used to my pronouns. But he does try.

'Yes, *they* seem okay,' I heard Flip say and I wanted to say, 'You don't have to put such emphasis on it, Flip' but it's a start. Now I knew they were now going to leave so I cut the Shrew loose and began to cut my way through the milling madding crowd.

They were all hot to trot. They were all looking for action. They were sick with it. They were so sick with it, you could smell the need come off them in waves.

I wanted to say: Just lower your standards and it will happen. It made me sick.

With jealousy.

I don't get much action because I'm non-binary. It's because they're all too confused to know what I want and I suppose I don't know what I want either. I'd like it all, a bit of this and a bit of that, and some of that as well. If you don't know what I'm talking about, I can only pity you for your lack of imagination and refer you to a dictionary. Look up the word 'euphemism' and let your mind roam. But not too much.

Because non-binaries seem to get a bad rap, right?

Happened to me. Last year. May explain my bad temper. May explain my cynicism.

There was a person who started to sweet-talk me. The person said that my aesthetic was appealing. I liked that. The person had made the compliment about my persona rather than about my person. And then I discovered that the person had gone around telling everyone that I was going to put out because non-binaries are all mad for it.

You can imagine who told me?

The Shrew.

I didn't believe it. I thought it was just hormones. Perhaps she had wanted what I had. And there was too much at stake for me to believe it.

This is now my rule: Don't tell anybody. Because I had made the mistake of telling Flip and Sin that I was expecting a guest for dinner and they had gone mad with joy because I don't generally have friends or such.

When the Person came over, they let us order pizza and made themselves scarce and even before the clicks of the door had faded away, the Person's hands were all over me. Of itself, this might even be seen as a compliment. Such passion. But then two things happened. I smelled the person and there was body odour. Now, I am not averse to body odour because it is a natural human smell and I want to celebrate how different and magical we are, this and that and these and those. But then the Person said: 'Make it happen for me.'

That was when I discovered that I was just a device. I was just a way to get off. I was Foras Road, Mumbai and I was Patpong, Bangkok. I pushed the Person away and said: Go home.

And the Person said: 'You're nothing but a tease.'

I wanted to say: 'No, right now, I'm just broken-hearted.'

I let it go. I let the Person go. I asked myself: What do I want?

I laboured over it and I made a list or a poem, I don't know:

You're out there somewhere
And you're interested in me.
You're gentle with me
You give me words.
You trust me with confidences.
You know I want it all.
You know I want it hot.

This morning I woke up and thought about replacing 'gentle' with 'tender' but it didn't work. Maybe it should be a list. If it's a list I can just say: Oh and gentleness too. Why can't I know if this is a poem or a list?

Then I added:

You smell of cinnamon and bitter wormwood.

Where was I going to find someone like that? No, not a list. A poem. A poem can be about what doesn't happen and what can't happen. A list is too bruising. I'd like tenderness but gentle will stay. But when I read it, I will know that gentle means 'I want tenderness' but it didn't fit in the line. Now I was in the middle of the prom and there was the history teacher bleating: 'So glad you came. Come and sit with us.'

This is the ultimate insult. Come and sit with the teachers. What could I say but 'I'll be all right.' I turned and headed to a corner of the room. I have about thirty per cent of my sight left and it's enough to get me across a room without bumping into too many people or things. I knew where I was heading: the store room.

It's just off the gym and it's quiet and I can wait out this night and go home unscathed by ABBA. I mean, 'Dancing Queen'? Really!

I had a plan. I had my phone. I had Spotify. I had music. I would dance. I would dance for myself. I would dance for a formless, nameless, beauty and we would make beautiful music together and live happily ... no, no, we would be together for as long as the music lasted and when it stopped, we would walk away and ...

I started thinking about this and I began to think it might be something to note down. But first to try it out aloud:

I will be with you
Until the music lasts.
I will be with you
For the hum in the blood.
For the song in the pulse
I will be with you.

I will be with you
For the aria of our waking together
For the concerto of our days
For the opera of our lovemaking
And the lullabies you will sing.

I will be with you
But when the song fades
As songs all must
I will walk away
And you will too.

Out of the darkness of the storage room, a voice spoke.

'Promise?' the voice said.

It was a husky voice, old leather and Velcro. I knew every voice in class. This was a new one. Who was it?

'What's your name?' I asked, and it was so stupid. I mean, there must be a hundred ways to come back to that one and I had to ask the most ordinary one.

'My parents gave me a shite name. I don't use it.'

'What do you use then?'

'You know the sign for infinity? That's my name,' they said. I didn't mind that I couldn't see them.

There would be time for that later.

'Lemniscate,' I said.

'Lazy eight,' they said. 'I like that version.'

'I'm @,' I said. 'Like the sign in the middle of an email address?'

'Pronouns?' the voice asked.

'They/them,' I said. 'Yours?'

'Same-same,' the voice said and then the person stepped out of the shadows. They were wearing a priest's cassock but one that had been worked over with graffiti.

'Read some to me?' I said, pointing to the words I could barely see.

'You read this aloud,' they said and showed me something that looked like a poem.

'I'm seventy per cent blind,' I said. 'Retinitis pigmentosa.'

'Damn your eyes,' they said sardonically and I laughed.

'As if I don't,' I said.

'Hold on,' they said and twisted around and then that old leather voice began:

Go on, break a poet's heart.
In the bloodfurrow,
They will grow roses.

What can I say?

For my next birthday, I got a tattoo: an infinity sign. Will a bloodfurrow follow? Who knows? But that's what keeps us going. Who the duck knows?

Such a Tease

K Vaishali

'I'm bored,' Blue Hair breathed into the phone. Her husky voice went lower. 'Can we do something fun?'

She is crazy for me.

'What do you want to do?' I asked.

'I don't know,' she said. 'Can we play something?'

'Like what?'

'Badminton? Carrom? Even Ludo would do at this point ...'

What a tease.

'I'll see what I can arrange,' I said, and hung up.

I'd put the call on speaker while drinking with Lala and the boys. They looked at me and grinned.

'What are you going to arrange, dada?' Lala ribbed.

'Some entertainment, of course,' I said, barely containing my smile.

'Just take her to the lake,' he said.

'The lake? She is a city girl. She won't do it by the lake. You have to treat city women with respect,' I said.

'Where will you take her then?'

'Probably to my old room at Uncle's house, since she's already staying there. Nobody uses the first floor anymore, so it will be quiet and—'

'No interruption,' Lala said, smiling suggestively.

I showed them a picture of Blue Hair. My cousin Charu had a picture of her and Blue Hair as her display picture. In the backdrop was the literature block of Sophia College, where they both studied. They were visiting the village for pujo.

'What do you think?'

'She is a little plump,' Lala said.

'You don't know anything, Lala,' I said. 'You waste your time chasing skinny girls when you don't know what the real deal is. You don't know the lengths chubby women can go to satisfy a man if you give them even a little attention ...'

'I should sweet-talk Charu then,' Lala said, laughing.

That comment made me furious. So furious, I stood up and pulled him by his collar. 'I'll break your legs if you talk about her like that,' I warned him.

'I was just joking, dada! Relax!'

I let go of him.

'So, is tomorrow going to be *the* day?'

'Not tomorrow, maybe later this week,' I said. 'You have to take it slow with city girls. They want a mental match as much as a physical one. But the tease is as good as what is to come. Poor Blue Hair is bored. What will she do for entertainment in this dull old town? She needs me to show her a good time.'

After another round of drinks, I crashed with the boys at Lala's house. In the morning when the boys took off for college, I decided to skip and go to my sister's house so that I could take my four-year-old niece, Lumi, with me to Uncle's house.

Chicks love guys who are nice to babies.

Blue Hair was sitting on the verandah reading a book, wearing tight, ripped jeans. I sat next to her and played a game on my phone. She didn't look at me at all at first. It was all part of the teasing that got me excited to be near her. We'd been silent for half an hour before she finally looked up from her book.

'Nice highlights,' she said. I had just gotten red highlights. It made my curls glow in the sun. Blue and red—we'll go together like fire and ice.

'I want a bottle of whisky. Where is the nearest wine shop?' she asked.

Oh, she's a slut, all right! Whisky should get her wet and loose.

'You can't just go to a wine shop here,' I said. 'It's dangerous.'

'Why? What will happen?'

'Girls don't go to wine shops in small towns. Ask Charu, she'll tell you,' I said. 'Men like me are there to get liquor for you. I'll get you a bottle tomorrow, and we'll drink.'

She sighed.

'I'm saying this for Uncle's sake,' I said. 'I understand how free you girls are in the cities, but here it's different. It's better if I get it.'

Lumi ran into the verandah and climbed onto my lap. Blue Hair sighed again and returned to her book.

She is not a baby lover; I should take Lumi back.

I asked Blue Hair, 'Do you like Chinese food?'

'Yes! I'd love some chowmein.'

'There is a small restaurant in the market area that has good chowmein,' I said. 'Want to go?'

She nodded. By the time I got Uncle's car out of the gate, she had invited Charu and Lumi to come along.

What a tease.

In the car, she sat in the front seat, which meant she wanted to be entertained by me. I kept looking ahead but, while changing gears, my fingers gently grazed her knee through the ripped jeans. She felt my touch and didn't move her leg, didn't even wince. I changed gears a few times needlessly, just for her to enjoy herself. Suddenly, as I was changing gears, the gear stick got stuck. When I pushed it with force, my hand slipped from the gear stick and hit her knee. She moved her feet away.

Why didn't I hold the stick tightly? It was going so great, and now I've messed everything up. How will I show her now that I'll be gentle with her?

At the restaurant, she sat next to Charu, leaving me with Lumi. They locked eyes and held hands, talking amongst themselves as if the world around them had stopped. City girls share everything with each other.

I think Charu is sleeping with Blue Hair's brother. Why else does she bring Blue Hair to this town when she's so bored here? She wants Uncle to see how good Blue Hair's family is so they will accept her brother as their son-in-law. It's a weird move, but she can't outsmart me. I bet she'll come with the brother next time. She says she and Blue Hair share a room in a flat, but I bet they all probably live together with the brother and other guys.

I dropped them home and Blue Hair said the sweetest 'thank you' with a wide smile. It made my heart flutter.

***

I bought whisky that night. A bottle of Antiquity—blue bottle whisky for Blue Hair. She was reading on the verandah again, wearing a loose T-shirt and cream sweatpants.

Her thighs are so juicy, I could bite into them.

She smiled as I walked by. I like her smiling face when I'm the reason for her smile.

I took a bath and came out to the verandah in my towel, hoping to get her to look at me. I made a show of drying my clothes on the clothesline so she could note my taut biceps, but she didn't look up. Still in my towel, I pretended to water the plants so she could spot the creases along my clenched butt. Not a peep. She just continued to read her book.

What a tease. These city girls play hard to get.

Lumi came running at me shouting, 'Where is all your chest hair, mama?'

'Shhh.' I covered her mouth. Thank god Blue Hair didn't notice.

I made chilli chicken for her to eat while we drank. It was the perfect night for entertainment. Charu's grandmother was visiting for the night, which kept

Charu and Uncle busy. Blue Hair was alone, near the fire pit, looking away. I invited her for drinks, and we went to my old room on the first floor. I told her it's quiet there, and we could watch a film while we drank.

'You must be so proud of Charu,' she said. 'She worked so hard for that fellowship.'

'I don't believe in all that,' I said. 'I am not doing any fancy degrees, but I have this village's respect. I ask one of the boys to do something for me, even if they don't want to, they'll do it. I think that's more important than fancy titles and money.'

'Okaaay? But that doesn't mean you can't be proud of your cousin who is doing so well,' Blue Hair said. 'She topped our class last semester.'

'Charu's a smart girl,' I said, taking out the whisky bottle from the bag. 'Is Antiquity whisky okay?'

Blue Hair nodded as she browsed through the TV channels looking for a movie. The room had a single cot in one corner facing the TV. She sat on the edge of the cot.

I poured some of the Antiquity whisky in a glass meant for Blue Hair. While she was not looking, I grabbed the bottle of Blender's Pride from behind Auntie's sewing machine and poured some in my glass.

I wouldn't have any money left if we both drank Antiquity.

After thinking for a minute, I poured some Antiquity from Blue Hair's glass into mine and some Blender's Pride in Blue Hair's glass.

This will make our drinks look the same.

I also took a quick swig of the Antiquity so the bottle looked emptier.

'Find anything good to watch?' I asked, turning towards her.

'I had no idea there were so many cable TV channels. I only watch Netflix.'

'I have Netflix on my phone,' I said, handing her the drink. 'Sit comfortably.'

'Thanks!' she said without moving, still sitting on the edge.

'Show me a picture of your brother,' I said.

'Why?'

'Just. If I know what he looks like, I won't accidentally beat him up if I ever see him.'

She looked confused, but she searched on her phone and showed me a photo of her brother. He had raggedy hair and looked very much like the type of scoundrel Charu would sleep with.

'So, does he live with you?'

'No, he's doing his master's in Delhi,' Blue Hair said.

Yeah, right!

'Be honest, do you have a lot of parties in the house?' I asked.

'Not unless you count hosting book clubs as parties.'

Quit playing, Blue Hair!

I crawled onto the cot and sat facing her with my back to the wall. Still a lot of space between us. She didn't move. She barely looked at me. She kept looking at the TV and sipping her drink.

Why is she so shy? Is she still mad about what happened in the car? Or does she think she doesn't have a chance with me? I should say something to show that I'm very interested.

'You know, I really like chubby girls,' I said. 'Ask Charu.'

'Okay …?' she said, eyes still on the TV.

On an impulse, I spread my legs wide. I was wearing tight jogging pants, and it was easy to notice my bulge. She couldn't possibly ignore it. I was sure she'd notice it in a second and get excited.

Look down, come on, look downward.

'I'm hungry. Think I'll go downstairs and get dinner,' she said, getting up. Without looking at me, she placed the drink on the floor and dashed out of the room.

'But you just had one drink—' She left before I could finish the sentence.

I drowned in the bottle.

Ugly piece of shit. Thinks she's too good for me. Bitch!

Just the Two of Us

Aravind Jayan

I

Naveen International Hotel. The name came to him when he heard that his classmates, Bijith and Sneha, were looking for a place to spend Valentine's Day. Naveen's parents would be away that weekend. The wedding invitation had been lying in the living room for months. He would be home alone.

Naveen drew a logo—*NIH*—with a coconut tree sprouting from the 'I' on the margins of his notebook. *5-star stay. Deluxe service. All are welcome.* He thought about this for the whole of the Malayalam period.

By lunch break, Naveen had made up his mind to help. Feeling nervous, he went up to Bijith and said, 'You can use my house if you want. My parents are going out of town. No one will be home.'

Bijith played for the Kerala U-19 cricket team. In the school hierarchy, Naveen was low-class and Bijith was royalty. They'd never really spoken to each other, so Bijith seemed taken aback.

'Really? Just like that?'

'Sure. If it helps.'

Bijith closed his tiffin box, looked around, and casually asked him a few questions: Where did he live? Was it a big house? How long were his parents going to be away?

Once Naveen answered—haltingly—Bijith said, 'Well, thanks for offering.'

He shook Naveen's hand and smiled, but that was it.

Two days passed. Two days during which, Naveen supposed, Bijith looked elsewhere for a place and found nothing.

Finally, he came up to Naveen on Thursday, at the end of chemistry lab. 'Is your offer still open?' he asked. Naveen could see Sneha in the distance pretending to study a volumetric flask.

'Still open.'

Bijith took down his number and address, and then, before walking away, slipped him a hundred-rupee note. 'Just to say thanks.'

'Anytime,' Naveen said. He stared at the money and smiled.

***

Naveen had always wanted a girlfriend but no girl seemed to want him. At seventeen, he'd proposed to so many people—batchmates, seniors, juniors, a junior's cousin—that he'd earned the nickname 'herpes'.

It had started one day when the maths sir was doing a sex-education seminar. Pointing to a chart about STDs, he'd said, 'Some of these infections spread easily from person to person, and they are very hard to get rid of.'

From the back of the room, a voice had called out: 'Just like Naveen'.

But the nickname was dated now, Naveen often told himself. He had changed.

A year ago, he had even come close to finding someone—a girl from his maths tuition. They'd chatted on Facebook for four months and it seemed they might go on chatting forever.

Then one day Naveen's parents checked his phone. They read three messages where he was complimenting her dimples and one where he was asking for a selfie.

'Is this what you do at tuition?' his mother had said.

After an hour of insisting that the whole thing was only an innocent friendship, Naveen shouted, 'And even if I were in love with her, is that such a crime?'

His mother had threatened to call his teacher. His father had brought out his report card.

By the time Naveen was sent to his room, he was asking himself why he'd even bothered to make his parents understand. Of all the people in the world, why would *they* understand *love*?

Naveen felt that his parents were a miserable couple. They'd been married for nineteen years. Most days he didn't understand how they were together.

Not only were they always fighting, but they also seemed to have an agenda against every particle of romance.

Naveen's mother, as head of the PTA, had once complained about the girls in his class wearing too much make-up. They were being a distraction, she'd said. She had also written to the principal about seeing a couple sitting too close together at the canteen. It had led to an email about decorum.

As for his father: when, earlier that year, news about hotel raids had flashed on TV and the police paraded college students in front of the camera, he'd said 'shameless' before lecturing him about the importance of waiting till marriage.

* * *

After finding those messages, Naveen's parents had taken his phone away for five months. They'd informed the girl's parents too. She switched classes to the evening batch and Naveen never saw her again.

In any case, he now satisfied himself with daydreams. He had also grown fascinated with the few couples in class, foremost among them, Bijith and Sneha.

Bijith and Sneha had been with each other since the eighth grade. Like Bijith, Sneha too was popular, as a dancer. Together, they would have been perfect in a snow globe.

How wonderful, Naveen often thought, to have someone like that.

He also observed the transit of secret notes from desk to desk, and the giggling and handholding during breaks.

Sometimes Naveen felt like an old man watching young love and recollecting his romantic past—a past he'd never had, of course.

Other times he felt angry. Annoyed too—on top of being called herpes, he'd now gained a reputation for staring.

* * *

The following afternoon Naveen's friend Vinay heard about his offer to Bijith. Vinay wanted him to set up a camera in the bedroom.

'100 rupees is an insult,' Vinay said. 'Give me a chance. We can live-stream for a few people and charge 2000 rupees per head. No recording. No one needs to know. I can make sure.'

Undoubtedly, Vinay was a creep. He was also Naveen's only friend. It wasn't that Naveen liked him; his own low status in school meant he could only socialize with other low-status people.

'Money is not the point,' Naveen said. In his head, a voice announced: *love is.*

He looked in the direction of Bijith's desk. Bijith was unwrapping his lunch box with great care. A smile flashed between them. Naveen got goosebumps.

And while Sneha didn't smile at him, he sensed a softening deep within her face when they made eye contact.

Sure, Naveen had never been part of a couple. But in a sense, wasn't he part of one now?

Over the last two days, Naveen had started to feel like Cupid. Who was Cupid but a single guy who selflessly made love happen for others?

Actually, maybe Naveen was even more important than Cupid. While Cupid made people fall in love, he'd never helped them find a room.

'What *is* the point then?' Vinay snapped. 'Why are you helping these people? Sneha is a bitch and Bijith is an asshole. Last month he told everyone I give hand jobs to PT sir. You know he started that rumour, right? They look down on us.'

Maybe they look down on you, Naveen thought.

He felt magnanimous. He also felt Bijith and Sneha's gratefulness, their warmth, shining on him from afar.

Later during English period, Naveen drew another logo in his notebook. *NIH.* And in beautiful cursive: *Where there's always room for love.*

If Bijith and Sneha had a good time, Naveen thought, maybe he could do this more often somehow; maybe he could start a haven for couples.

***

On Valentine's Day—that Saturday—Naveen woke up happy. By the time his parents left, it was eleven.

Naveen texted Bijith.

'House is free :)'

'Roger that. Coming soon.'

This reply delighted him; it felt like they were on an undercover mission.

Quickly, Naveen got to work. His own bedroom was too cramped so he'd decided to use his parents'. He began by gathering all the dirty clothes that were strewn about, putting them in the laundry bin, and then pushing the bin out of the room. Mood killer.

That done, he decided to change the sheets. From inside the cupboard, Naveen found one that was satin red, spread it over the mattress, and tucked it neatly in the corners. He changed the pillow covers too. In the end, it might have been the best bed he'd ever made.

Naveen could have stopped there, but suddenly, he wanted everything to be perfect.

From the garden downstairs, he plucked roses, pulled out their petals, and threw them over the bed.

Nothing but the best at NIH, he thought.

In the living room cupboard, he found a scented candle covered in dust. *Cherry Blossom and Sandalwood.* He set it down on the bedside table, closed the curtains just so, and lit it carefully with a match. Then Naveen connected his laptop to his father's speakers and chose a playlist called 'Made for Love'.

He was getting a plate of snacks ready, thinking he'd share it with Bijith and Sneha over small talk, when his phone rang.

'Hey,' Bijith said, 'We'll be there in thirty minutes.' There was a lot of background noise, mostly laughter. He heard Sneha's voice say 'forty', which Bijith repeated.

'Okay,' Naveen said. 'Sounds good.'

'So where will you leave the key?' Bijith asked. 'Under the doormat?'

'The key?'

'So we can get in.'

'Oh I'll just open the door. I'll be here.'

There was silence. Sneha's voice said: 'What, no. That's weird. I thought no one was going to be home.'

'Listen,' Bijith said. 'I told Sneha no one would be there.'

'Right. No. My parents aren't but—'

Bijith sounded agitated now. 'Could you maybe leave for a few hours and just keep the key under the doormat? Is that okay? Because otherwise, what will you do? Just stand around?'

'Right.' Naveen stared at the flickering candle flame.

'Hello?'

'Yes.' He took a deep breath. 'Okay, I can do that.'

'Great.'

Then just before the call ended, he heard Sneha saying, 'And tell him to change the sheets and all that, I don't want to catch herpes.'

The line went dead.

* * *

Two minutes later, Naveen was sitting on the floor. His body was shaking and his eyes had welled up. He felt like an idiot.

The phone rang again.

Naveen decided he would tell Bijith that something had come up and the plan was off. Only, it wasn't Bijith calling; it was Vinay.

'What are you up to in the evening?' Vinay asked.

Naveen stayed quiet for a long time listening to him speak about some online tournament.

Finally he cleared his throat and said, 'Can you still do the livestream?'

If Vinay seemed surprised, it was only for a second. '100 per cent. We'll share the link with a few people, that's it. Just need your phone camera. Set it up, turn it on, hide it, and come over quickly. I'll tell you how.'

II

Anil and Prema were thirty minutes into their car journey when Anil gasped and said, 'Where's the gift? Did you forget the gift?'

Prema was in a bad mood as it was. She had no energy to say, 'You were supposed to take it. I told you.'

Instead, she stared out of the window as Anil turned the car around. She sighed.

Lately Prema had been feeling distant from her family. She suspected there was something wrong with her son—he was so anxious and sad all the time.

As for her husband, he didn't even seem to see her.

Valentine's Day made everything worse. While Prema had never cared about it—even abhorred it these days, such a crude display—the rest of the world clearly couldn't get enough. TV shows running special episodes, discount coupons printed with Cupid's picture like he was some deity, cafés decorated with heart-shaped balloons. In some ways she felt everyone was celebrating what should have been a day of respectful mourning.

It wasn't like their marriage had always been dry though.

Prema remembered a Valentine's Day from when they first got married. Anil had toyed with her, pretending to forget, and waited until evening to surprise her with a room at the Meridian Hotel. There, he'd given her a bouquet of roses and a giant gift basket. They'd fallen on the bed holding each other, laughing. She'd thought about Julia Roberts in *Pretty Woman,* which she'd seen at a theatre in Kochi several years earlier.

Prema looked at her husband, who'd finally stopped frowning at the road. She sighed again.

Back when they'd just got married, and before Naveen was in the picture, he had done so many small things for her: bring her sweets from his walks, or, on Saturdays, insist they go for dinner at *Garden Grille.*

And even though Prema felt utterly embarrassed—even furious—about missing *any* of these juvenile things, lately she'd overcome her ego enough to drop hints. She'd done a lot of it just that week, in fact.

'Do you remember our first Valentine's Day?' she'd asked on Monday, feeling like an idiot. 'You surprised me so well. You set it up perfectly.'

On Wednesday, she'd described something a man in her LIC office had done the previous year for his wife. 'Can you believe it?' Prema had said. 'She was so happy.'

And on Friday: well, by Friday, she was irritated with all those Dairy Milk commercials featuring showy, teenage couples. She'd still said something to Anil about how beautiful the roses in their garden looked.

Anil had nodded at each of these hints, though clearly nothing had sunk in.

That morning in the car, he'd turned the radio on, settling on a station playing romantic songs. This had momentarily given Prema hope. To what end? She didn't know. She noted that Anil was happier than usual. God knew why. Maybe because he was getting a break from their son's moping, or from home-cooked food. To her, though, he talked only about the traffic. This Anil did passionately, while also snapping at a driver here, instructing another there. Prema felt so angry—at her husband for letting her down despite all the hinting, and at herself for expecting silly gestures—that she could have jumped out of the car.

By the time they returned to the house, Prema had sighed some twenty times.

'Go get the gift,' Anil said. When she stepped out, he added, 'Actually I'll park. I need the toilet.'

The best Prema could do was ignore this and walk ahead.

* * *

Something was off. Unlocking the door, the first thing Prema noticed was that instead of smelling like that morning's breakfast, the house smelled nice.

'Naveen?' she said. There was no answer.

This itself wasn't unusual. She was always scolding him about headphones. Prema turned around and looked for Anil. He was still parking.

Slowly, suspiciously, she scanned the empty rooms on the ground floor and then followed the scent up the stairs. Now she heard music coming from the master bedroom; a soft keyboard, the steady beat of drums, a voice singing:

To make those rainbows in my mind
When I think of you sometime
And I wanna spend some time with you

Just the two of us
We can make it if we try

She paused in front of the bathroom and looked in. It was empty, as was Naveen's room.

'Hello?' Prema said, quieter this time.

Walking up to the master bedroom, her heart was pounding. She hesitated.

When Prema finally opened the door, it felt to her like she had entered a painting.

The clean room. The red bedspread. The rose petals strewn across it.

The perfect slant of late morning light came through the gap in the curtains.

She stared at the scented candle. It was the very same candle Anil had put in that gift basket their first Valentine's Day. *Cherry Blossom and Sandalwood.* Prema took a deep breath. The smell flooded her brain. She remembered the bed at the Meridian Hotel.

Before she knew it, her eyes were full. All that rage Prema had collected inside her melted into relief. She shuddered. A smile appeared on her face.

He *had* listened.

Prema felt such a powerful rush of emotion that when her husband walked in five seconds later, she pounced on him with a kiss so forceful and passionate, *he* was the one who looked surprised.

Prema thought, *Good.*

She started ripping his clothes off. The music swelled.

Just the two of us
We can make it if we try
Just the two of us

Prema slammed the door shut and pushed her husband on to the bed.

'Happy Valentine's Day,' she said, climbing on top of him.

The Friends

Suniti Namjoshi
(from *Feminist Fables*)

And so, they walked through the woods; summer was over, but the sun was still warm, the leaves were turning. They chucked stones into the water and likely looking sticks. They competed amiably. It never once crossed their minds that walking through the woods in early fall was an ancient pastime for heterosexual lovers, which, even for them, might have much the same meaning. They said, 'Good Night,' and met two days later at a formal gathering. They drove off together and got themselves supper, they exchanged stories. They had a great deal in common: an extreme ambition, a preference for women, and a happy wit. Each was charmed by the other's gentle-ness and felt at ease, they parted cheerfully. Three days later they met once again. They had done some thinking. They were still cheerful and kind and friendly; but about what they had thought, they said nothing.

Sitting on the Porch, Watching the Trains

GANKHU SUMNYAN

As soon as the man entered the compartment, I sized him up. My first question was: Can I beat him up? Or would he? The odds were stacked against me; he was tall and burly; strong shoulders; *huge* forearms.

The habit comes from my hostel days. A list ranking the strongest boys to the weakest would regularly make the rounds. I could, given some leeway here and there, count myself somewhere in the nebulous middle point—not very strong but not very weak either. I was constantly afraid of sliding down the ranks.

The man had come in from the pretty station the train had just stopped at. I had already started thinking of how I would describe it to Sofie. I would tell her about the station as well as this large, awkward man who was standing before me, clearly looking for a berth to share.

'Can I sit with you till Karakavad?'

He adjusted his glasses while talking, and I noticed clearly the reticence and the worry. Hassled. In a hurry. His strength was only an appendage.

I couldn't say no, though I should have because I didn't know how far Karakavad was. And his request was an interruption in what had been a pleasant journey so far—the moon-lit early-winter night, the good dinner, the quick run of the train and the pretty stations. Most of the compartment was asleep, the travellers down in their bunks and off to whatever thoughts and dreams quiet nights in trains allowed. The family opposite my berth was also out and I could hear some gentle snoring. It was probably the father who had offered me some dried snacks earlier, which I had refused because I didn't want to appear too sweet or too friendly. I was still learning a few lessons in those days—how to be, how to behave, how to think. Still a convalescent out in the sun after a long time indoors. And Sofie was the sun.

Or nearabouts. Bright glow. Bright smile. Cheery. Quirky. She was my classmate in the pre-university college I had joined after years out in the wilderness of boarding-school blackouts and tough-loving parents. She was someone who found me interesting, someone who would listen to what I had to say and reply, and laugh. Basic things but life-affirming. In her presence I felt perfectly adequate, that I didn't have to be a 'man' or that I was lacking in some important attributes which was what had gotten me sent to boarding school.

No, I didn't want any more tough love. I wanted soft Sofie love, with all our weirdness mixed together. I was sure we would eventually end up there, with the way things were going.

Foolish of me to think that way, perhaps, but who hasn't extravagantly believed in the perfect destiny of their loves?

He sat down and introduced himself as Mukul. Even showed me his ID card, as if I were the TT. And then he leaned back against one end of the berth. He seemed a size too big for the berth and had to significantly pull up cartilage, muscles and bones to fit comfortably. But once done, he seemed snug. As if he was used to doing this. He had already started appearing funny to me, because I imagined describing him to Sofie and making her laugh.

He told me he was a photographer, currently working on a project to document seasonal flowers in the Deccan Plateau. Ah, the man just fit into the prescriptive parameter of things I liked telling Sofie or things that made her laugh—a big man working in a very delicate job, huffing and puffing all over the Deccan Plateau with his big-soled boots, camera bag and rucksack, from which emanated a faint smell of sweat, soil and flowers. You could accidentally even catch some kindness in his eyes if light hit his glasses at the right angles.

The project was part of a bigger government undertaking, he said, and began to fiddle with his camera. At this point, he sat with one of his legs folded underneath him, and another stretched down on the floor.

'I have been walking most of the day,' he said, and smiled at me, almost apologetic.

Then he showed me the photos for which he had walked all day under the sun. The flowers were very pretty and very small, growing in clumps in the crevices of the rocks or near abandoned quarries, where their thin but tough roots stretched towards the rainwater collected in the hollows. They were hardy and couldn't be easily killed.

I understood the passion in him, and imagined myself working in some such demanding but fulfilling job in the future. But I also felt great that I could match his passion with the glow in my heart about Sofie. Because that was also a passion, right? I had almost started to tell the man about her but stopped. My heart bubbling with untold feelings, I looked out of the window and secretly wrote the letters of her name on the windowpane.

While I was caught in such romantic entanglements, the man stretched his left leg fully on the berth, right by my side. He sighed with relief but I was shocked. Shocked at the trespassing, the transgression.

And now that the leg was there, it seemed like it would stay put.

How far was Karakavad still? Shouldn't I have clarified all this before giving him the berth? What was I going to do now? Questions raced through my head.

The day after the journey, when I was telling the story to Sofie and Vinay, Vinay nodded gravely at this particular point. He was the boyfriend Sofie had brought along to meet me at Central Mall. She wanted us to be introduced to each other, and looked very proud as Vinay and I shook hands.

Vinay was from another school, a year senior to us. He was already a published writer, well on his way to becoming something. Tall and with a hint of a beard, he looked very much the scholar he was. And it didn't seem possible that with his serious look and serious voice, he would ask someone out, but that's what he had done with Sofie a short time before I came into the picture.

So where did that leave me? No doubt I was in some way relevant to her, but Vinay-level relevant? Definitely not.

I put on a brave face, keeping the shock in check, and focusing with all my strength on Vinay while telling the story. I had meant to tell it to Sofie but I was afraid that if I looked at her, I would break down or shout or lie down in despair. Which wouldn't be very manly of me.

Back in the train, I had to reimagine and redraw the picture of my co-passenger in my head. What he did had changed everything. The other leg would follow, I was sure. Because that was the final position to be achieved, wasn't it? I imagined him doing the same thing again—I would be looking somewhere and whoosh, the other leg would be on the berth in its entirety, as if it had always been there, as if it was meant to be. It was as if he was making me wait for it—looking outside the window, taking gulps of water, touching his camera now and then—and all the while his right leg, the one that did the heavy work, the one that gave him a sense of balance and authority, the one keeping an eye on the ground like a crab on the ocean floor, waited impatiently to be brought up and put to rest.

The gall of it! The trickery!

Sofie narrowed her eyes here. She didn't agree with my assessment of the man. 'Or he was just tired,' she said.

Vinay shook his head in some confusion. He didn't know which side to take. But he seemed to depart from Sofie's opinion about the man, smiling slightly at her remark. I liked how invested he was in the story, how interested.

In the train again, I looked at every twitch of the man's right side, aware of every slight shuffle he made. So much so that I realized I was staring at him. I turned away and wondered whether this was how battles felt—the crabby moves, insidious thoughts, the neuroses about the enemy, the desolation of the battlefields, the sheer unwillingness to back down and to put everything at stake.

And there, I could see the slightest movement of the left leg, pushing a little inside. *Please don't do it,* I pleaded in my thoughts. It almost touched the end of my jacket. The strategic moves had begun, and I was a defenceless town running around helter-skelter, not knowing what to do or if it was even possible to do something. Or was there probably an understood compassionate ground due to which what he was going to do was already allowed? And right before my eyes, I saw the right leg being raised slowly, like a large truck appearing on the crest of a hill, bearing down slowly and slowly onto the field of vision till it was rumbling in faded chrome, paint, and black smoke right in front of one's eyes. His left leg had come down with a thud onto the berth and I had imperceptibly moved, without being asked to, as a repercussion of what I had been unable to do, of the defeat that was already inflicted upon me from the first moment he appeared.

It had to happen, didn't it? He couldn't sleep with his legs dangling on the floor, could he? I reasoned with myself. My eyes closed, I felt the rhythmic tread of the train's wheels, my body as if a part of that rhythm too, floating over the same track. In that acceptance, my co-passenger reappeared as I had first imagined him—as someone benevolent, a bear-like celestial traveller come down to Earth, like Ursa Major.

'That's a great thing,' Sofie had said. 'I mean, I know it would have been difficult for you, but at least a good conclusion, without much rancour.'

Vinay had closed his eyes and given a deep nod, putting himself right where I was, imagining the man in the train as the celestial bear.

'I am sure this is not the end though, is it?' he asked. 'Because you travelled with him the whole way like that? Did he get down at the place he mentioned?'

At this point, Sofie had become a little nervous, sighing and looking away in nervous anticipation.

I had made peace with the log-like legs beside me and I had even been able to drift off to sleep. But soon I felt something hitting my knees again and again, which, mind you, were still buckled and folded underneath me. It was my co-passenger's left foot that with each jerk of the train swung like a pendulum and struck my body. The man was asleep of course, oblivious to what was happening. He harrumphed and shook his head from time to time, or rubbed his nose, but he was asleep, travelling in his own dreamland. The distance between us appeared huge, not only because of the physical contortion I would have to perform to reach him, but also because I could not bear to think of waking him up with gentle pats or by calling his name. 'Mukul, Mukul, wake up, you are violating my space' didn't sound right to me.

'But you could have,' Sofie said, leaning forward.

'No, it's hard to do that sometimes,' Vinay replied. 'We are hostel boys. It's awkward.'

I was getting more and more irritated with the man. I looked outside the window to find some peace. To no avail. No moral standards or lessons of maturity prevailed. What prevailed was my hatred towards my own ineffectuality, my passivity, that I was unable to do anything about the situation for so long. No Ursa Major anymore, no celestial traveller. But a violator who took advantage of other people's graciousness.

I tapped him on his leg to wake him up. Nothing happened. The legs had gone dead from lugging the large man and his equipment on the Deccan Plateau trails. I hit harder, to no avail again. The train's swaying frame probably masked my force. Could I hit him harder? Could I slap it? Or shake it?

Sofie's eyes rounded here, expecting something terrible.

I felt I had reached the limits of decent behaviour with the man. Like I had done my part and wasn't responsible any longer. But the foot kept hitting me, and at one point, finding it much easier to completely rest than balance itself constantly, it eventually parked itself on my thigh. That was it.

I grabbed the leg and threw it over, probably with more force than I had intended. That sent the man sideways over too, crashing down onto the floor with a loud *aah* and waking everyone up. Lights were immediately turned on, and the child on the opposite berth started to cry.

There was the man, balancing himself just above the floor, with his left hand on the berth, like a humungous spider caught in the act of spinning its web.

'What's going on?' the father from the opposite berth demanded.

'He threw me over,' the man said weakly, trying to get up from the floor.

'You kept hitting my leg!' I countered.

'When did you come in? Do you have a ticket?' said a man from the next cabin.

The man trembled a bit as he got up, surrounded by accusing eyes. 'I am travelling to Karakavad. Only an hour or two from now,' he said.

The father threatened to call the police and told him to leave the compartment. He also threw me a disgusted look when he learned I had allowed him to sit on the berth. Ursa Major or Mukul happened to be not so fearsome after all. In fact, he quietly put on his boots, mumbling he meant no wrong, and before leaving the compartment, raised his hand in an awkward apology.

Then he was gone.

'That's it?' Sofie had asked. 'He was gone just like that?'

That was it. The man was gone, leaving behind a deep sense of awkwardness and regret. On my part, that is. I felt that instantly. Felt I could have treated him better.

Sofie spoke with some feeling. 'We really shouldn't judge people by their appearances.'

'I don't think so,' Vinay replied gently. 'I think you did the right thing. Yes, you have regrets and all, but only in retrospect, right? What if the man was really a weirdo?'

'Couldn't have been. His intuition,' Sofie pointed at me, 'at the end said otherwise. The man was just tired, that's all.'

Vinay didn't agree, but said nothing. And all of us were lost in our own thoughts. It was the soft evening of the previous day again. Lamps were being turned on, and the water fountain started to gush a few metres in front, emitting rainbow lights. More people started to appear on the sidewalk of the mall, but they were in half-light and as such their personalities were muted and less affecting. Everything that had happened in the train could only have been a play of light—the big bear in reality muted and soft but made to appear harsh and deceitful by his tiredness, by the lights inside the train. If I had spent a day with him walking the Deccan Plateau, and seen his frailties and strength, maybe I would not have thrown him off the berth.

Anyway, the story was just a story. It had happened, and it had become a story. And the telling of it was a way of reaching out to someone now immutable and far away, someone going gone *gone*. I don't think Sofie knew. Or maybe she did. She was very good at intuiting things like that. She looked at something far away, probably still thinking about the story, as if sniffing out further threads, further branches, pugmarks of other journeys; and I had the smallest hope that one of those threads would lead back to me, to why I had told the story.

Vinay wondered what really was this project the man was a part of and whether he could write something about it.

'Only no one would read it,' he said wryly.

I would, I promised.

And I would look for the feeling of a big man trying to do a hard but delicate job. I would look for the feeling of the wind blowing across the rocky hills, of coming across sudden clear ponds and lakes. I would look for the depiction of the lives lived in small towns with small stations. And for the small moments when hearts went on a spiral at the sight of little houses in the dark far away, and of thinking nothing would be better than sitting on the porch of one of those little houses with someone you liked and watching the trains pass by.

Michael Pandiya

Meera Ganapathi

'Michael Pandiya is the powerhouse of the cell,' Arumugam droned as my eyelids grew heavier and my doodle more detailed.

Who was Michael Pandiya now? And what did he have to do with cellular organisms? I looked up from my rendering of Arumugam's luscious behind (elephantine in my doodle, complete with a tail) and glanced at the blackboard that had 'mitochondria' scrawled in chalk and underlined three times.

MitochondriaMichochondriaMichaelpangea. Oh. Okay.

The bell rang, and Arumugam glared at me. 'What are you writing? ShowmeShowme dear, just show me no,' he said with the righteous passion of one who longs to flay you. I closed my exercise notebook with one hand and scratched my head with the other, in a manner I hoped looked helpless or foolish, both of which could pass off as innocent. But Arumugam was relentless; he was now walking towards my desk with every intention of yanking my notebook open. I could feel perspiration pooling in my armpits, which is when I heard a trembly voice say, 'Arumugam!' with some authority.

Our principal had entered the room to make an announcement. And mercifully for me, Arumugam had to stall his premeditated murder for the richer purpose of discussing the school's Annual Day.

'Six Heads is out to get you,' AB informed me needlessly.

Six Heads was Arumugam, a (very) literal translation of his name in Tamil.

AB and I were walking back home from school having finished our dance prep for Annual Day. My cycle had a puncture, and AB had sweetly left her cycle in the parking lot to give me company on my way home.

We were both a bit tired after practice, having done seven rehearsals under the unrelenting eye of our physics teacher, Mandakini Miss. Unsurprisingly, I was assigned to be one of the male dancers, complete with a bristly moustache, and AB, the female lead.

AB is gorgeous. Her hair cascades down to her waist in long, silky waves She has dimples—not ordinary dimples but cheeky ones that flit and disappear at the hint of humour. Her skin glows from within, even without her TikTok Vaseline slugging hack. But her nicest feature is her bow-shaped lips. OMG. Her lips are *beautiful*. They look like, you know, they're almost alive, like they're talking to you even before they frame any words she has to say. Sometimes her lips land in a blinding smile, sometimes they seem mildly bitchy pulled up at a corner, judging you just a little, and quite often her lips settle into a thin frown that accentuates her dimples so you never really feel threatened by her anger but you're aware that you're crossing a line. And this one time she was yawning, I swear, she was just yawning and she looked pretty because her mouth made such a perfect 'O'. Ugh, I know, I sound like I have a crush on her but, I don't. I mean … wait, more on that later.

By comparison I look … sturdy. Even without the comparison everything about me is average. My smile is all right but nothing to write home about. My hair has good days but I keep it tied so what's the point. Even my eyes aren't like main protagonist stuff; they are sort of watery and mid. I have strong legs but they can seem manly. I have planned on dyeing my hair white in streaks to give myself some 'chutzpah' (a word Pappa likes to say often). But as of now, I don't have the will or the wallet.

'I heard mitochondria as Michael Pandiya,' I guffawed, hoping to extract a laugh out of AB.

I was gifted a snigger.

'Me too!' she chortled, and I watched those charming dimples dart across her cheeks and then settle in deeply.

'You heard Michael Pandiya too?'

'Yes! And guess what—we actually know a Michael Pandiyan in Nagercoil,' AB said, slapping my back with her palm before dissolving into laughter and I had to hold my stomach and laugh—it was so hilarious.

Six Heads has the weirdest accent; it sounds Texan and Tamilian and often leads to the strangest word associations. He's probably never been to Texas but biology is delightful thanks to him. While explaining the reproductive system to our much-amused class he once cried, dramatically, 'Silence, you savages! Sex is a holy thing!' That fuelled a storm of laughter, as you can imagine.

By the time we reached my building, our laughter had petered down to smiles. I turned around and asked, 'What are you doing later? Want to watch *SpongeBob* at mine?'

AB looked a bit uncomfortable. 'Ummm ...'

'Never mind,' I said and scooted upstairs, my cheeks hot with a mix of shame and annoyance.

I think I heard her say 'sorry' but I didn't have it in me to turn around and clarify.

I'll have you know that I've received a love letter. Yes, me, who is mid at best. The letter was scented and everything, and it arrived in the middle of English class in the hands of a fourth-standard boy. I honestly found it charming because the boy said, 'For Miss Rehina Rosario.' (Yes, I am possibly the only Goan in all of Koturpuram.) I said 'Thank you' very graciously and resisted opening it till lunch break.

Unsurprisingly, during lunch break AB was the first one to lean over my shoulder as I opened the letter at my desk. I could feel her hot breath in my ear and pushed her away playfully. 'Relax!' I said, smoothing the letter with care as she tried to paw it open. It was a short letter, written with a simple black gel pen. And it went like this:

Raina,

You're not like everyone else. No one else here reads Bleach, only you and me. I liked you the moment I saw you outside Britto's. I liked you even more when you smiled at me in the lab.

Text me if you like me back.

Arvind T.
(9950783271)

He'd spelt my name wrong and I hadn't smiled at anyone in the lab. But my mind flashed back to Arvind T. He was tall and skinny and quiet. Some girls found him cute. I ...

'Raynuuu ...' AB spoke for my brain as usual. 'He's perfect. Imagine, now you, me, Dhruv and Arvind can hang together after school! I miss you so much when I'm there. Just text him pleeeeease!'

I decided to text him because I guessed it was about time I joined the others at the park where couples and older kids hung out after school. It's just that I didn't really feel excited or anything. And I badly wished I did. I wanted all the symptoms of a crush: flutters and sweaty palms and rapid heartbeats and anything, really! So I tried to force myself to feel something by going through his Instagram to confirm his cuteness. But I could only manage slight contempt for the spelling errors in his captions. And on close inspection, I found that his eyes were too close together. Honestly, all I felt about this letter was relief at being included in a place I didn't really belong to.

That evening, I made AB cancel her plans with Dhruv and type out my texts for me. She lay sprawled on my bed thinking hard before sending each text, even though there was nothing particularly interesting about anything she was saying. In fact, she was rather excessive with her emojis but if not for her I'd have nothing to say at all. Arvind seemed sort of annoying. All he could talk about was hanging after school, about how I should try leaving my hair loose and the way I'd smiled at him. Bro … when??!!

That night, long after AB had left, I scrolled up and down the texts she had sent posturing as me and I felt sick inside. How would I speak to this dude when I actually met him? None of AB's texts sounded like me. I zoomed into the four hearts she'd sent and oh no, no, NO! I'd accidentally sent him a GIF of a cat slurping a bowl of ramen. My stupid fat thumb! It was 1 a.m. Shit.

I was thinking of you too—came the lightning-quick reply.

Yuck I was not. My hands felt clammy as I typed: *lol.*

What are you doing?

NM. Lying in bed, I typed, instantly regretting this statement because of course he asked me—

What are you wearing?

* * *

I wear my mom's old nightie to sleep. It's a blue batik printed kaftan with embroidery at the neck and deep pockets into which I jam my phone and a Vicks Vaporub for sinus emergencies. It's very ugly. It's very comfortable. But I wasn't telling some creep from D Section anything about my nighttime routine. For four days after the 'what are you wearing?' text I ghosted Arvind. He texted me day and night asking me what was up and how I could 'crumb' him that way. I had no idea what crumbing meant and I had no interest in finding out either. Arvind was relentless. Unfortunately, so was AB.

'What is the matter with you? Don't you want a boyfriend?'

I didn't reply. We were at dance practice as usual. The others were learning to skip their feet in a delicate giddha arch but AB and I were down by the steps of the stage, taking a break to drink water.

'Raynu?'

'I don't know...I'm not feeling it.'

'Feeling what? He's so cute! Everyone likes him and Dhruv says he's super chill and funny. In fact Dhruv said ...'

'Dhruv says, Dhruv says ...' I mimicked her.

'What is that supposed to mean?'

'Just that having a boyfriend doesn't make you special. You're like every other teenage girl in the history of the world! Stop making me feel like I'm missing out. I'm not.'

AB gaped at me, her beautiful mouth hung open, wordless. For once she looked just plain stupid.

* * *

We've made up since then, obviously. I'd sent a text saying I didn't want to be pressured into dating someone I didn't like. She said, sure, she understood. But there is a slight wedge between us. Especially when she leaves every evening to meet Dhruv and the gang of people who hang at the park with their dates. I pretend to be okay, but I feel a crushing sense of shame or sadness when she leaves and I watch *SpongeBob* or sketch every evening to pass my time. We have been joke-reviewing old sitcoms for years now and *SpongeBob* started out ironically but soon became a comfort watch. In fact, AB even named her cat `Gary' after the snail in the show. I suppose there is something steady and grounding about SpongeBob and his lack of ambition.

Anyway, Mama thinks we're fighting and keeps threatening to call AB's mother to find out what went wrong. But this will blow AB's cover so I just tell her to 'not invade my privacy.' I have plenty of stock phrases borrowed from a clever website called 'Therapy Speak'. I once tried 'my body, my choice' while wearing a unicorn-shaped plush onesie to Sunday mass. But I got threatened with 'my money, my choice', aka no pocket money for a week. My dad enjoyed the whole thing I can tell you. First, he guffawed at my onesie, then at my mother's diabolical comeback.

I digress. My family is cute. There's nothing wrong with me, inherently, I have not (yet) been messed up by cold, unemotional parentses. They are very warm and considerate if anything. I just am that way on my own, you know? Like, I feel NO desire. Nothing makes my heart race or skip a beat and I am not curious about sex or boys or kissing. In fact, I think I find it gross.

I suppose this is my roundabout way of telling you I don't date a guy because I don't want to. What's wrong with me?

***

AB looked sad on Monday. We were cycling to school and I noticed that she was unusually quiet and had forgotten to wear her regular cocoa butter spritz. I'm ashamed to say I saw her sadness as my chance to dislodge the teeny wedge between us.

'What's wrong?'

Sometimes I imagine AB to be a hot water bottle. You know the kind your mom keeps under her butt for her sciatica? Anyway, she's always full to bursting and if you just happened to open the mouth of that bottle, hot water will gush out. What I mean is, she has no qualms about telling me EVERYTHING.

'Dhruv watches porn.'

'Ugh.' My bike actually veered a little.

'I watched a bit to see what he likes about it.'

'Yikes. Wait, wait ... let's park.' We found a quiet spot under a few mango trees in the colony. We'd be late for school but this was worth being late for.

'Yes, I hated it and told him not to watch it again.' AB said, looking a bit embarrassed.

'What did he say?'

'He promised me he wouldn't.'

'Do you trust him?'

'I don't know ...'

'What? Why? I don't love the guy but he seems like he's really into you.'

'Hmmm ...'

'WHAT?'

'It's just the way he kissed me the other day.'

'You've *kissed?*'

AB looked at me strangely. 'We kiss a lot actually.'

'You ... never told me.'

'I didn't want you to feel bad.'

Somehow that made me feel worse but I didn't want to show it so I adjusted my tie and said, 'Okay, so how does it feel ... to umm ... kiss?'

'Magical ... it's sort of ... magnetic.'

'How do you do it?' I asked, genuinely curious. You see, I find the very thought of saliva exchange unhygienic.

'It just happens, you come close together and it seems like it's all you are meant to do ... I can't explain it, you'll have to try it yourself to know. You'll have to feel that way about someone, powerfully attracted. You know?'

I didn't. I was just crushed that I didn't. Still, I put these thoughts aside momentarily because I remembered that AB was upset about the way Dhruv had kissed her.

'What was wrong with the way he kissed you?'

'He kind of grabbed me and it wasn't romantic … just harsh.'

'I'm sorry,' I said, hugging my friend.

* * *

Annual Day is tomorrow and a bunch of us are doing rehearsals in the OAT (Open Air Theatre). It's a giant open grassy field filled with plastic chairs facing a large stage with deep blue curtains in the background. During each performance a painted set drops to provide a backdrop that suits the performance. Ours is a rendition of mustard fields in Punjab, presumably plagiarized from the movie *DDLJ*. In our performance, a troupe of us are meant to enter the stage with pots on our head and in my case, a bundle of hay. The dance is meant to depict the harvest season in Punjab. I don't understand why the teachers couldn't allow real boys to dance with the girls and instead humiliate me, Deepika and Arati, who are also flat-chested.

Anyway, the song is a village melody and it's rather beautiful and today we're rehearsing with our costumes. AB is meant to sashay in at the end with me. But I have asked for a ten-minute break because I have my period and my cramps are killing me. So I sit back in the third row and try to view the dance like an audience member would. I watch with pride as AB waltzes in, wearing a yellow salwar suit, her long hair in a thick braid, dimples flashing, hips twirling ... I have eyes for no one else, she's so beautiful. Life would be so easy if I were gay, I could console myself with being secretly in love with my best friend, but I am not attracted to her either. I just admire her, I suppose.

And last night while thinking of AB kissing I felt a heaviness in my chest. What if I never wanted to kiss anyone, ever? Would that be okay? I kissed my wrist softly, my mouth teasing the soft skin on my hand and fell asleep in that odd posture. When I woke up this morning, my neck hurt and I felt that same heaviness. What does one call this?

* * *

It's Annual Day morning, I'm all set in my bristly moustache and white khadi kurta, a yellow turban perched on my head. AB looks stunning, and I look handsome, I suppose. Our troupe takes a group selfie. I pretend to be manlier than I am and everyone laughs. My phone buzzes.

I look at a text from Arvind that says: *cold bitch.*

I ignore it and AB looks at me curiously but I don't tell her what's up. We do our last-minute make-up touch up. Or rather, the girls do because us boy-girls literally have nothing to do except check that our moustaches haven't fallen off. The song comes on and I hike my hands up in the stereotypical 'balle'. My dad must be somewhere in the audience, ready to have a good laugh mixed with misplaced pride. We sashay in, our feet in tune with the dhol, big smiles plastered onto our faces. As it goes with these things, my eyes scan the crowd for my family. I spot a hand wave at me from the fifth row, when something large, cold and solid hits my face and knocks the breath out of me. I stagger for a second and freeze.

I can't see anything for a whole minute. No one notices me stop, until Leher bumps into me irritably. 'Mooove ...' she says. I can't, I'm frozen and there's something warm and wet on my face. I touch my face and see blood on my fingers. My nose is hit and suddenly, pain comes at me in all its cruel force.

Someone from the audience screams at the sight of my face with blood dripping down. I sit down because my legs are buckling under me. The dancers pause, and I'm ushered backstage.

***

'I should have continued dancing,' I tell AB later. We're curled up on the couch in my room watching *SpongeBob* on my laptop. Patrick is scarfing down smoked sausage, when she leans in and wraps her right arm around me, bundling me inside her, 'You were in shock.'

'Who would do such a thing though?' she wonders out loud.

The facts as they've been deciphered so far by the school administration is that a bag of cold ice was thrown at me by someone within a group of boys standing close to the stage. None of the boys is owning up or giving up the name of the culprit, even though they all know who it is. The whole bunch of boys has been suspended—there are eight of them. I am horrified—what have I done to inspire such hatred when I mostly keep to myself?

But the bag of ice reminds me of something. I tell AB about the 'cold bitch' text from Arvind. AB's face is ashen. 'It's not just Arvind then, it's also Dhruv.'

'What? Why?'

She nods angrily. 'I ended things with him and he blamed it all on you, called you a cold bitch.'

'I don't know what to say. Why me?!'

'He's too conceited to blame it on himself,' she says with a sad shrug.

'Are you okay? Didn't you really like him?'

'I was wrong about him, Raynu. He's not who I thought he was.'

I look at my beautiful sad friend, and hold her close. Her mouth droops and still a dimple manages to sneak out. It's such a lovely mouth really. She looks at me looking at her and we have a moment, I suppose. Because right then, she kisses me, all of that full lush mouth, all over my lips. I let her, I am so curious and so hopeful.

'That's what a kiss feels like,' she says when we're done.

'It's ... sweet?' I manage to say.

'It's anything but sweet, you idiot,' AB guffaws. We both laugh and hug in a mad rush of joy.

'You still have your moustache on by the way.'

'I love you,' I tell her. And I do. It's not that kind of love but it's some kind of love.

About the creators

Andaleeb Wajid is a hybrid author, having published nearly 50 novels in the past 15 years. Andaleeb enjoys writing in a number of different genres such as young adult, romance, and horror. Andaleeb's YA novel *Asmara's Summer* was adapted for screen to become *Dil, Dosti, Dilemma* on Amazon Prime and other works are in the process of being optioned or adapted. Her YA novel, *The Henna Start-up* is the winner of the Neev Literature Festival Award 2024, Crossword Book Award 2024, and TOI Auther Award 2025, along with receiving honourable mention at the BK Awards, 2024.

Anurag Banerjee (b. 1991) is an independent photographer based between his hometown, Shillong and Bombay. On a perpetual quest to define what home means to home, he self-published his first book *I'm not here* in 2022 which explored the conundrum of belonging to two places at once. His following books *The Songs of Our People—I & II* looked at identity and belonging through the lives of musicians in Meghalaya, while also asserting his belonging to the place.

Aravind Jayan is a writer from Trivandrum, Kerala. He won the Toto Funds the Arts Award in 2017 and was shortlisted for the Commonwealth Short Story Prize in 2021. His first novel, *Teen Couple Have Fun Outdoors,* was named a 'best book of 2022' by *Open Magazine, The Wire, Deccan Chronicle* and others. It was also shortlisted for the Everyman Wodehouse Prize for Comic Fiction, and has been translated into several languages.

Gankhu Sumnyan teaches English at a government college in Arunachal Pradesh. His stories have appeared in *Out of Print, Gulmohar Quarterly, Cafe Dissensus, East India Story,* and in the anthology *The Best Asian Short Stories 2021*. He can be reached at gankhu.sumnyan@gmail.com.

Jerry Pinto lives and works and writes and thinks and translates and eats and drinks and runs and ruminates and loves and hates and sleeps and rises and dreams and does and undoes and shoves and pushes and waits and watches and hopes and laughs and edits and verbs his life away in the middle of a city with many names by a sullen and grey sea.

(Image credit: Nishant Saldanha)

K Vaishali (she/her) is based in Hyderabad, India. Her memoir *Homeless: Growing Up Lesbian and Dyslexic in India,* published by Yoda Press and Simon & Schuster, won the 2024 Sahitya Akademi Yuva Puraskar and was shortlisted for the Rainbow Awards. She has a Masters in Communication from the University of Hyderabad, and she leads a team of documentation writers at a tech company.

Meera Ganapathi is an author and the founder/editor of the literary and arts publication, *The Soup*. Her book on walking, *How to Forget* was published by HarperCollins in May 2025. Meera has written various books for children, like, *The Girl Who Could Not Stop Laughing, Uma vs Upma* and *Paati vs UNCLE* (Puffin India). Her poems and short stories have appeared in several anthologies, including, *Cat People* and *A Case of Indian Marvels - Dazzling Short Stories by India's Finest Writers.* She

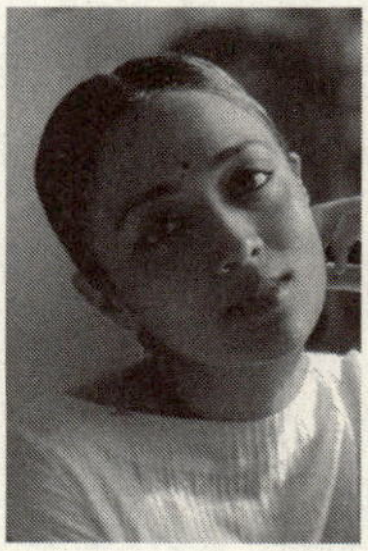

lives in Goa with her baby, her partner and her misunderstood cat, Apple.

Nisha Susan is the author of *The Women Who Forgot to Invent Facebook and other stories*. She is an editor and a translator. She always has homework and currently has exams.

Riddhi Dastidar is a writer and reporter who lives in Delhi. They have four cats and over fourteen tattoos. On the internet Riddhi is called @gaachburi.

Suniti Namjoshi is a fabulist, a poet, a satirist and a feminist. She was born in Mumbai, India and lives in the southwest of England. Her books include *Feminist Fables, The Blue Donkey Fables, The Fabulous Feminist, Suki, Aesop the Fox, The Good-Hearted Gardeners* and most recently *Matriarchs, Cows and Epic Villains*.